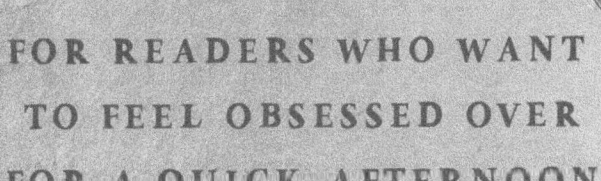

FOR READERS WHO WANT
TO FEEL OBSESSED OVER
FOR A QUICK AFTERNOON

I GOT YOU

Cover Designer: Charlotte Mallory
Interior Artwork: Charlotte Mallory

Editor: Heather Creeden and Erica Hearne

a novella

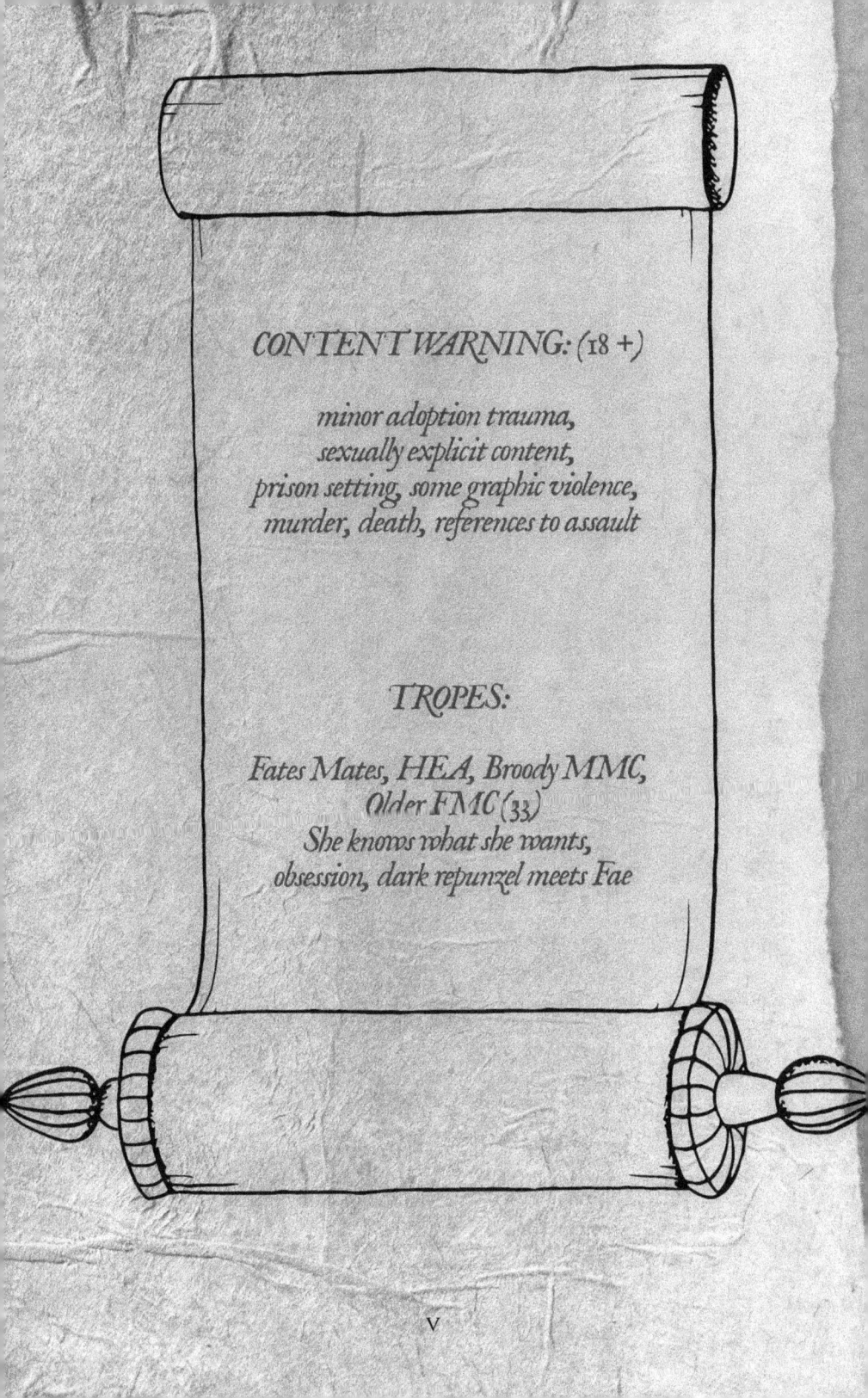

CONTENT WARNING: (18 +)

minor adoption trauma,
sexually explicit content,
prison setting, some graphic violence,
murder, death, references to assault

TROPES:

Fates Mates, HEA, Broody MMC,
Older FMC (33)
She knows what she wants,
obsession, dark repunzel meets Fae

Victoria

Chapter I

H ope is a fickle thing, like brittle bones before they *snap*.

All of mine have shattered into dust.

Perhaps it's time to be reborn.

I'll never forget the first time I sent *him* a letter; the sky had wept for the hundredth time that year, a sign of the *change*. Rain used to nourish the plants so the sun could warm the air and dry the drenched soil. Now it rains with a cold chill, the bitter air delivering frigid bites, the ground so wet that horses struggle to pull carriages. The skies always reflect this *change* when a darker tide looms in the air, like nature knows society is about to give.

Blood will be shed. A war, possibly.

It's why my mind is restless with theories, eager to escape from this place. The man who wants to call himself my father is dead set on marrying me off like

1

I'm prized livestock that's getting too old to be of value. There's still *just* enough time for political capital to be gained in forcing my hand.

He's clinging to his broken hope, too.

Crops are thinning. Nefarious creatures creep within the shadows of the woods. My sallow hand is what he's trying to offer, but I'm determined to yank it back…

Kane was a way out of all of this.

A deep inhale imbues my lungs with the scent of wet stone from rain that batters my windows. The wind always blows harder up in this tower, but it's a violence I've grown used to. Comforted by it, even. It not only rained the night I penned my initial contact to Kane, but it stormed.

An ominous promise from the fates.

Every rule had been broken by writing to Kane, every aspect of my future completely risked.

For *him*.

For some brittle hope I know better than to try and hold.

As I stare at the blank parchment on my desk, my reality spins like a weaver caught in a chaotic design. Why would I write to a man locked away in the Carrows? And not just a *man*, but the darkness that consumes the light—a High Lord of the Unseelie. A large behemoth that even the fiercest men in my father's ranks rarely speak ill of. Those cowards still refuse to whisper the name *Kane*, as if his shadow will somehow hear them.

My eyes move to the quill adjacent the parchment, then to the other letter, which is creamier in color. Rougher.

With *his* words scrawled on there.

Writing to him is like a curse. The second I slipped the initial letter to a confidant, I sealed my fate as another person who spirals around the words of Kane. So many follow this man who challenges the Seelie Highlords, the opulent rulers of our lands.

The same people who placed me in this tower.

I gently pick up what he sent me. In the previous letter that incited our discourse, I merely thanked him for what he had done a year and a half ago, detailing my recollections of coming across Kane in a tavern as he was traveling. How he scarred my father's right-hand man so badly, Lawrence now wears a partial mask, all because I'd been struck and left with a broken, bloodied nose. Kane had made *one* instance of eye contact with me, right as I looked up when I heard the commotion, still trying to collect my dazed mind. *Something* had flashed in his silvery eyes, and then...

And then, he refused to acknowledge me. That's when the prison cells of the Carrows consumed Kane.

Why did he do it? It's not like I can't heal my own bones, not with the powers I was born with. It's why they often hit me so badly. Kane even laid down his sword and let them take him, all the while it was painfully obvious he refused to meet my gaze again as my own nearly burned holes in him—looking back on it, I agree that he went with my father's men too easily.

So many whispers claim that he went to the Carrows on *purpose*. That he knew of my father's location and intentionally crossed paths with us. Perhaps my being struck was the excuse Kane was looking for to attack; he can hide his motives behind something that *appears* noble. Making eye contact with me was useless for his cause, like saving a mouse from a cat that he had no interest in.

He's planning something.

And like any bored woman confined to a tower, I haven't been able to stop thinking about him since.

Having Kane settled in a stagnant prison, one near my forced housing, is like having him captured inside a globe. I can safely debate my actions, hesitate as many times as I wish, and even not think about him if I so choose.

The latter hardly ever occurs, if I'm to be honest with myself. The man is a subject of my absolute fascination. A prisoner to his image, just as I am to this castle. Writing to him was an itch to scratch, like perhaps if I did it I could finally stop ruminating about him. I honestly didn't intend to hear back from Kane.

My hand twitches, eager to pen him another, like being near a flame but feeling no heat. How close can I get before the fire truly singes me? The Unseelie are not known as forgiving or easy to negotiate with, and he's one of the few I've ever come in close contact with. So why would I, the adopted daughter of a Seelie High Lord, write to our enemy?

I gently pick up the letter he had sent me.

Victoria,

I know who you are and which tower they keep you in.
You risk much by sending your letter to me.
More than you know... I have to admit.
Do not engage with me further.
Closing any distance after this would seal fate.

No name.

No *Kane*.

But I have to believe it's from him. It smells like him; I hold it to my nose once more, the scent already fading.

It's the damn scent that broke me in the first place when he was only a few feet from me all those months ago. His musk stained my lungs like carving permanent ink into my skin. It's not uncommon for my kind to remember a scent more than the rest. We are not like humans.

But this obsession feels different.

I had never been so *persuaded* by the way a man smelled…

Not a man. A high predator. Someone who scares the very soldiers who guard me. One that has been just as vicious as my own adoptive father, if not worse.

Definitely worse.

If Kane appeared at the bottom of my guarded stairwell, I would half believe the men watching my every move would flee, preferring to risk my father's wrath over that Unseelie High Lord. When Kane struck Lawrence, everyone fled *away* from my father, rather than defend him in a possible attack. My father had shouted in triumph that there was a reason to now imprison Kane in the Carrows. To which most of the soldiers were hesitant to obey orders.

But again, he didn't fight.

And I now hold a letter from him in my hand.

Surely, my fascination is simply born out of boredom. He is the leader of a court that's taking over—a society that grows like weeds under the moonlight, so when one wakes up the following day, the tendrils have already stretched further. No one can recall when the influence had struck so deeply, or how Kane took over with such ease. The only thing we know is that any battle he's in, he's always alive. Always covered and dripping with the blood of *others*.

He wears his scars like earned badges of honor.

I place the letter down on the wooden table. What's wrong with me? Every time my mind wanders with thoughts of him, recalling the strong angles of his scarred face, I'm always faced with some kind of internal praise. I'm like the sheep that continues to compliment the wolves, even down to their blood-stained canines.

I'm utterly hopeless.

Or, perhaps, bored. Unsatisfied. Lost.

Sliding into my slightly wobbling seat, I eye the blank parchment next to Kane's letter. An old window is my only source of light through the gloomy storm, and some of the candles are dwindling. Replenishing my supplies always seems to be an afterthought to these people.

What would responding hurt?

Surely, Kane was lying. Or manipulating.

It's what he does.

I can't even fathom the idea that writing a letter would *bind* us in some kind of fate.

And why would he care?

He's trying to get to me, to use me to get to my father. Maybe he defended me on purpose, too. To ensnare the bored woman kept in a high tower while enacting his other plans.

I grab the quill and dip it into a pool of violet ink, sliding the metal tip against the glass well to clean the drips. I have few things I enjoy in this life, and using this ink is one of them.

Violet is my most preferred color.

Seeing as I *loathe* the man I must call my father, I

don't really care if this fucks up any of his plans for my life. If anything, I might be counting on it.

Once I begin to write, I can't stop:

Kane,
    As much as common sense begs me to heed your words, I am afraid I cannot... at least, not with this letter. I have never, in my life, had someone strike my father's closest men for his ill treatment of me. Until you.
    I don't even understand why writing to you would seal any kind of fate.
    But you're right, nonetheless.
    This is probably pointless. No doubt your actions are convoluted, so there's not much to say.
    I don't know why I am responding right now. It's an itch I can't scratch.
    I suppose there's no reason to write this. My ramblings indicate as much.

I pull away.
Images of him standing above me after striking my

assailant infest my mind. It had been a night when my father took me on a bizarre journey, one that we never made it to our destination. Lawrence had been put in charge of me that night, as if I were some young maiden who couldn't read signs or think for herself.

Another fiber snaps from the rope that makes me who I am. Being *minded* like an adolescent. Women my age have had multiple children by now. I nearly drip purple onto the parchment from holding my hand in one place for too long, the little drop hitting the wood to form a bright, beautiful bubble of color.

I know why I rambled—I wanted to admit to Kane that he haunts me.

But under no circumstances does he need to know that.

Anyway, perhaps I am merely pulled to you because of the novelty. That would make sense. There's not much for us to discuss, either. So this will probably be the last.

Victoria

The words are completely pointless. Empty. Not even scratching the surface of what this man does to me. Of how I dream about him, much to my own frustration. How I have always heard terrible tides of the Unseelie and their darker magics. There's a reason why the Seelie have all but banned them from all of our lands.

No, I know why I penned him.

I want out of here.

If I cannot live within the light, I may as well embrace the darkness. Forge a new identity where I can have the friendships, love, heartache—all of it—that I crave. Silas, my *adoptive* father, never permits me to touch him, even if he fondly hugs his other children. I genuinely do not remember the last embrace I had.

Standing, I pace my room.

The room forced upon me.

It's a collage of gray stone, broken up by furniture that's painted the color of the sky, the fabrics a mixture of creams and fuchsias.

Regardless of what is best, I seal up the letter and place it within a book. Writing to Kane is tasting a part of freedom I can't describe.

The Carrows are allowed a rather lofty library. It's a prison colony island that the regents of our world will visit to acquire men or women to serve in their ranks. It's akin to visiting a pen full of rabid, wild beasts who are gifted freedom in exchange for their servitude.

Books still ship there, many desiring to have well-educated members within their ranks. Noble knights can only get so much done in a world that's overrun with corruption and death. A ruthless mercenary is sometimes the only salvation, and an educated one is even better. At least, sometimes. If they break that oath to serve, a bounty will be placed on their heads. One that's usually *too* lucrative to remain free for long.

If they fail, then the duskborn will hunt them down. They're the only ones of their kind that exist *among* the Seelie.

Kane is now among those people.

The candle chandelier above me shakes when thunder booms across the sky. I lie down on my bed, feeling a *change* happening. Perhaps I won't be here for long. I've lived here for over thirty summers.

Too long.

Something about Kane is haunting me, and I don't know what to do.

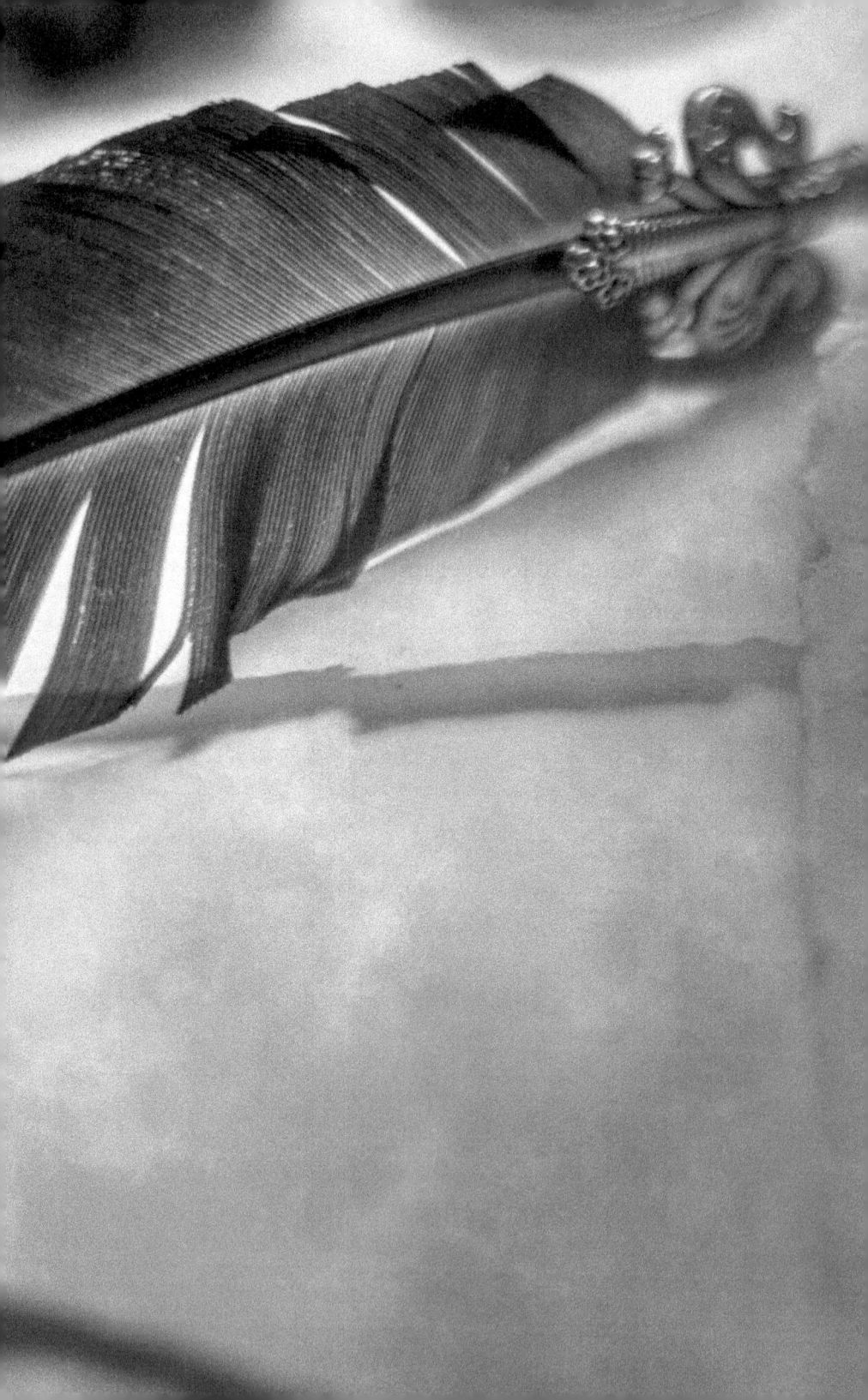

Chapter 2

Kane

The leaking drip of the storm breaches our stone walls.

It will be time to leave soon. Gather the collected followers and liberate those improperly sent to live on this island. It's the way with any damn dynasty —they grow too large and the first time true opposition approaches, paranoia grips their hearts like a fucking vice until cells overflow with the souls of the damned.

Souls I can *reap*.

Chaos always brings an opening for opportunity. *Many* will gladly join my side who are stuck here, and then it will be time to return to my court and fortify before the *change* occurs.

The Seelie will be culled. Those here will see to it. My freedom this time will unhinge the High Lord of these lands. *Her* adoptive father.

I grind my teeth.

They imprisoned her, too.

The metal chalice in my hands, one I stole from another when I first arrived, nearly bends as I stare blankly at the wall ahead. The thought of *her* inside those walls, being sent to marry herself to another—something they will force soon—given the need to solidify alliances...

Keeping her from my mind is proving to be more challenging than stomaching the gruel they call food here. And yet I have to consider her. The ramifications. How can I allow her to rot away in that tower like a forgotten delicacy?

My gaze focuses on the rows of bookshelves that surround me, old and broken in many places. She's a distraction when I should be honing my mind and searching for the answers we need in this fucking monstrosity of a library.

It doesn't change that I'm a slave to waiting for *her* letter to appear, should she have ignored my words—

My breathing stills when Osman enters my vision, the sound of stiff wheels echoing against the slate floor as he begins his task of returning books to their shelves. The Carrows is vast and houses upward to five thousand prisoners, rotating the libraries between each wing. Because the powerful and rich tend to search for vicious members within these walls, they permit learning and training of the body; a prison encampment designed to grind out the weak so the strong may be chosen. Freedom from here is earned through being bought to serve on an agreed-upon task.

If I were to be bought now, then the duskborn bred and born to serve these halls would hunt me down until they could drag me back.

Although not *me*… I could leave if I so wanted.

But I'm in here for a reason.

And while I have many of my own men with me here, we keep separated. Independent. I've made it clear that we act truly imprisoned until it is time—

I smell a female approaching.

Human.

Glancing her way, she keeps her dirtied head down and sits across the table, strands of brown hair parting in clumps from lack of washing.

"You're Kane…,"

Only silence answers her.

She fidgets, dirty fingers with grime-filled nails touching each other as she keeps her gaze down. "Please. I've been waiting for you to appear at this hour for over a week. I'm willing to offer my body in return for your protection. Especially if the rumors are true..."

There are many things one can say. I see the sad situation for what it is, but she isn't speaking to a savior of a benevolent kind. I've lived through atrocities that have numbed me to the pains of this world. Survival within the wastes that the Unseelie have been forced to live within has evolved us into something ruthless.

I'm here to reclaim our fucking throne, not save everyone.

"No."

I also don't appreciate her speaking openly of the rumors that I *do* plan to escape. The guards of the Carrows were easy enough to sway once I knew what to offer…

Her breathing quickens, and I know speaking a word to her is only inviting further noise. "One of your men, then."

"We don't openly use bodies as payments. Flesh becomes addicted to flesh too easily, and loyalties are swiftly corrupted."

Her cracked lips wordlessly open, wiping the greasy hair out of her face that may have once been pleasant to look at. "Please, I thought—I thought *surely*… I mean, *thank you*, for answering me, first of all. I don't want to appear ungrateful—I just don't trust the others… *you* don't hurt the innocent."

Facing ahead to watch Osman, I ignore the woman. The *change* will ravage the lands, and this prisoner; feeling pity for all is a waste of focus. Just because I don't target the innocent doesn't mean I'm their monolith, either.

"Then train me, or something." She offers in my peripheral, leaning closer, the table slightly moving. "You have women among your group as soldiers. I can learn."

Continued silence from me.

If she truly wants to offer herself, she'll know Freya recruits the females.

Small, desperate sounds escape the woman as if one of them will morph into words that might sway me. She clearly must know *of* me, because she sighs and leaves with a scoot of her chair, her shadow moving as she passes a torch. If I avert my attention and ignore who is speaking to me, it means leave me the fuck alone.

That woman *may* be useful, but what she clearly hasn't grasped is that I do not trust *offerings* of loyalty. That is earned by bleeding for it, and even then, I know the hearts of mortals are fickle. Her efforts also unfortunately come at a poor time for her, as I cannot pull my attention away from listening for the wheels of the book cart. They're advancing on the appropriate aisle.

I watch as Osman nears me, his once sun-kissed skin is exceptionally pale—a sign we've been here for far too long. He avoids eye contact.

The surge of curiosity that floods me pisses me off.

This is idiotic.

Indulging in any of this is disastrous.

Osman knows to stay away except for when he brings a letter from *her*. A slave to whatever hypnotizes me, to the promise of what it *could* be... to thinking about how they have the audacity to leave her high and away from the world.

My blood heats at the idea of them giving her to *any* man, which they will be forced to do if they want to strengthen their already weak unions.

It's *that* thought that brings me to my feet, staring at each book that Osman carries, wondering where *her* letter is. The letter that belongs to me; the *scent* of it that is mine to claim. Osman slides another book onto the shelf, but upside down. A hundred thoughts flow through as I stare at the binding, possessed with the need to possess *her*. To claim her before the others do, to liberate her and offer whatever she needs to truly taste freedom, like she is a special plant I'm careful to cultivate.

As there will be no freedom from *me*.

It simply will not work that way, and I know it. Any action on my end to take her from that castle will push me to stalk her shadows.

Osman's short hair has reached the half-inch length it usually does before he shaves it off; a ritual I perform every few days for myself. His voice is bleak and without emotion as he mutters, "I'll return at dawn."

Without another interaction, the man wheels his books to another shelf.

Turning my head to stare at the upside-down, worn spine with *her* letter inside, my mind is pulled in so many directions. We have a purpose here, a goal to liberate half of those within, *enlisting* them. And here I am, ignoring duty. Obsessing.

No, she is another kind of duty. But she cannot free herself of me if I shorten any distance toward her. Is that even fair?

I run my finger along the spine, my skin calloused against the smooth leather. Grit lines around and underneath my nailbed, the black ink of tattoos on my forearm blending in with the grime.

Removing the book, I grip it tightly. To send a letter back, I place one in this very book, and Osman will reclaim it.

With my gaze ahead and surveying, I slowly hold the pages to my nose, first greeted by the scent of parchment and leather. Her scent is incredibly trace, but *there*.

I'm suddenly infuriated that she is indulging.

What is she doing? Is she always this reckless? I'm not a kind, or gentle, man. I will ravage her, my instincts impossible to tame. Her softness is a divine reprieve, an escape I have yearned for but no woman has assuaged. A prize I've earned for the sacrifices I've made for my people.

Is the princess who wastes away in a tower aware of who she is? Of what fate will demand from us?

I breathe slowly with the intent to home in on *her*. My blood warms with a primal obligation. Her scent is like blood in the air, and I'm a starving beast.

I won't be able to back away now.

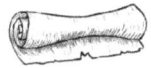

WITHIN THE CONFINES of my cell, I lay the book on the only table—almost a little too rushed—and flip through the pages until they stop…

I stare at the letter with a violet wax seal of a V, my chest rising and falling to a rapid rhythm, aware of the complexities that are slowly untying. My instincts purr to release the discipline that's honed me, desiring to indulge in what's *mine*.

My dirtied hand smears dark stains on the cream parchment of her envelope, making me wonder if all she's ever known has been a clean, uncomplicated world. Victoria's tower has held her back from the violence that molded me. My court would permanently alter her life and all she knows. Corrupt her ignorance. The souls that follow me have no decorum.

My breathing deepens when I open the envelope, staring at her handwriting etched in more violet—the only color I've seen in years, outside of the books. She has a tendency to accentuate the curves of *f* and *h*, and the basal voice within tells me that I can protect her from our damaged reality. Her heart will break as she sees the suffering of many, and then she will return to our den where I will fuck her until she forgets the rest... until she's drenched in my scent, and that will comfort her. *I* will comfort her.

I re-read a section:

"I don't even understand why writing to you would seal any kind of fate.

*But you're right, nonetheless.
This is probably pointless."*

She has no idea, does she?

I must burn the letter and all traces of it—breaking my better judgement, I smell the parchment *itself* before even realizing it, like an animal that knows its dinner will be removed before it can sink its teeth in.

There are traces of her, deeper, and hinting at her *true* scent.

My fingers dent the parchment.

Everything deepens. Instincts that could eviscerate those who would dare get too close. Maul any man who touches her with greed. They may look, as *anyone* would desire her. Only my scent will physically keep them at bay. Does she even know what she is? *Who* she is? How far do I have to unravel her before she can properly put herself back together after all that's been inflicted on her? What damage will that do?

The damage doesn't matter if her mate soothes her…

Those instincts grab my heart with a vice grip, telling me who I am to her. What I owe her. How she is lost and reaching out to me, even if she doesn't understand why.

Nearing the only window in my cell, I stare out at the raging, frigid sea, thinking of her. Of what it might feel like to claim her *completely*.

21

She will *reek* of her mate.

She is reaching out to me, and doesn't understand why…

It's the thought of her distress, and seeking out my help in such vulnerability, that makes me write to her again. After penning my reply next to a singular candle, I run the closed parchment along my neck.

She will want the scent.

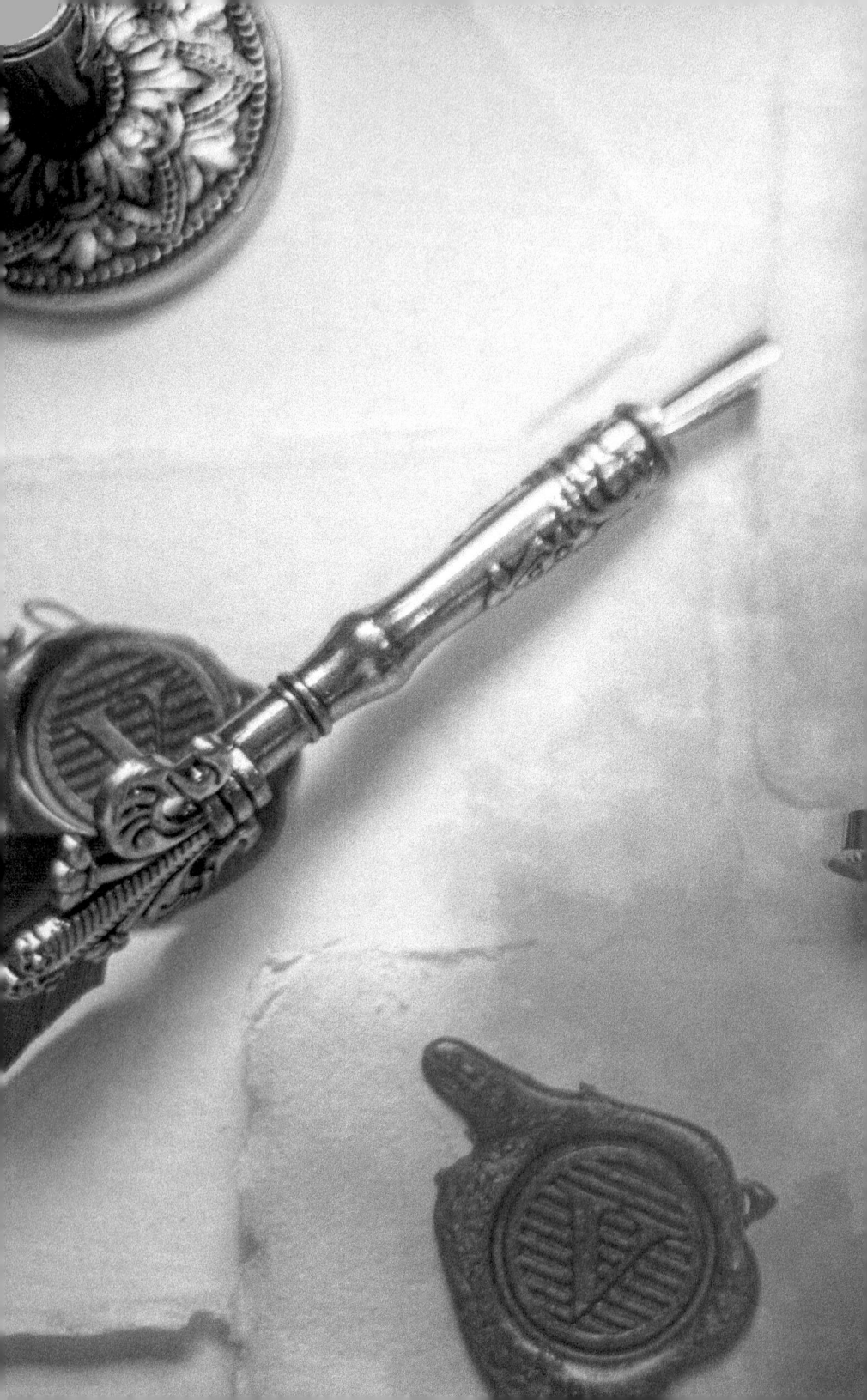

The anticipation of his reply haunts me in ways that have me questioning whether I should bother reading the letter if he writes again. This is no longer something rebellious to piss off Silas, the man who claims he has a right to me since he took me in all those years ago.

I'm *obsessing*.

As I pace in my towered room, the one that's simultaneously my escape and my confinement, I step on the hem of the simple blue dress that my lady's maid helped put on. Staring at the fabric, I'm lost in a sea of decisions that thrash against my identity crisis. But I also feel pretty in this mockery of an outfit, and I hate myself for it. I *always* have.

Is *that* why I like writing to Kane? Because it will make Silas angry? That seems so inelegantly simple. I've

25

lived through many seasons of emotions and revelations... surely I am beyond such behavior?

A knock comes to the door, and I jerk my head up.

"My lady, it's Ginger," says a muffled voice through the door.

"Come in," I reply with a clipped tone.

My lady's maid enters, her black hair tightly wound in a bun so perfect, there's not a single rogue strand. I've known her for nearly five years now, her fingers masterful at fixing any and all fabrics. She bows her head. "The High Lord requests you."

The annoyance at his request grinds against me differently while I'm on edge, waiting for Kane's reply. "What is this about?"

"He didn't say, my lady."

Sighing through flared nostrils, I know his *summons* can't be avoided. "Yes, fine."

Ginger's soft green eyes smile at me; she takes pity on the situation I find myself in. Genuine sympathy, too. So many in this castle take issue with my attitude, as if I'm a pet that needs to behave. But Ginger understands.

I still feel like a woman who has yet to experience her first bleed. No agency. Treated delicately. Despite my ability to endure, to be beaten and forced to heal myself. Over and over.

I need out of this tower, my heart ravaging me with temptation to break out of this damn place. Maybe it's desperation that calls to me, because I know my time is limited before Silas forces my hand—leaving here, under my own circumstances, is something I'm willing to die for.

Maybe *that's* what Kane means to me.

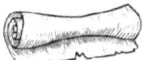

STANDING outside the High Lord's study, I'm transfixed on the gilded doorknob. Silas is currently speaking with another as I measure my breathing measured trying to prepare for *any* conversation.

After tucking a loose strand of ebony black hair into one of my many pins, my gaze drops down to the floor, my ribs restricted by the tight fabric. There's an edge I can't shake, as if I've been over-sharpened and continuously cutting on accident. Does someone like Kane live in a place like this when not in the Carrows? Does he wait for people to enter his space? Command a certain authority?

Where would *I* fit in a world where Kane ruled? Become a commoner? Would they mock and abuse me for being connected to Silas? I'm so rarely afforded a glimpse at a world beyond here, forever stuck in exploring what's beyond these walls through my imagination. Most of why I know is gathered through conversations and books.

The door creaks open, pulling my attention from my thoughts. It's a Lord to a neighboring province, one that owes allegiance to Silas. I study his comely face, a Seelie male with a pointed nose and eyes so lidded he always looks half-asleep. Someone I was poised to marry once.

"Oh, *Victoria*," he drawls out, his manners forcing him to conceal the depths of his judgement.

"*Lovely* to see you, too, Brom," I say with an annoyingly pleasant smile.

"I hear you're as unwed as ever," he chides, the door shutting completely behind him.

"Never been happier." I maintain my smile.

His thin lips curl into a sneer as he walks away, a placid guard standing against a wall coming to life in pursuit of his Lord.

Turning back to the door I dread entering, I extend my hand to grip the knob, inhaling with purpose before pushing open the heavy door. Pristine gardens are framed like a painting within giant windows, the woods lining everything like a living fence. I love the forest views down here versus looking at them from above. It's so nice to feel *among* the world, not towering over it like someone who doesn't belong.

My heart races when I spot Silas standing behind his desk, his back to me. Burgundy fabric clings to his lean body. His short blonde hair is greased back, a style I've come to loathe just for the association alone.

"So..." Silas begins, his arrogant voice grating

against my ears. "Your last potential suitor has rejected you. It's in that scroll on my desk. And I don't mean the one that just left this room."

"Oh, that's a shame," I lie, not moving an inch as I wait to hear whatever brought me here.

He slowly turns to reveal his slightly aged face, the lines rather deep for a male nearing eighty summers; one of the reasons humans are subjects to the Fae, as we live long enough to bear witness to multiple generations. And as of the last five centuries, it's been under Seelie Fae rule.

And Silas's rank sits *just* below the Supreme Sovereign, his lands, and those that owe him allegiance, stretching like a border wall along Unseelie territory.

"You are lucky I don't throw you in the Carrows for how *useless* you are to this family." He sneers so maliciously that his fangs are on full display. "A complete waste of our resources. That's all you've been."

Poised and collected, I hate showing him that his opinions wound me. "I understand marriages can align lands, High Lord. But it's difficult when I've never felt even remotely welcomed in this family. If I'm such a waste, then set me free."

"It's not a part of the deal," He mumbles. "And I need your worthless hand to secure marriage; to fortify for what's coming. My territory will be first attacked, so there's no question if *you're* going to help ensure I claim as many resources as possible. It's the least you owe us for all the decadent food, fine silks, and the lavish roof over your head."

The *deal.* Something he frequently references and never explains, and always says is why I've been given the life of a princess, even if treated like a prisoner. The thought of Kane writing to me, of touching against a power that's not this man in front of me, makes me feel like, for once, I might have an escape. A *real* one. "Who gives a damn about whatever darkness is coming," I say, Silas's shoulder stiffening as I let out everything without caring about repercussions. "You're confused as to why I am so hard to marry off? It's because I am *tired* of living in this secrecy. You hate me for a deal that's been made on my life, yet don't tell me what it is. You *never* have. You hate that your wife took me in as her daughter. You—"

"Do *not* bring her into *any* conversations."

"Well, she's a bit relevant since she's why I'm here. The *change* is coming, no matter what we do, and it's because of *her* that I'm stuck in this castle, ready to be utilized as a pawn for a family who doesn't want me. *Terrific* life."

His jaw trembles like he's holding back a hundred words, languid eyelids rising as he stares across the room.

I was never told why they took me in, other than Dahlia refused to give me to another home. My main regret in life is not knowing a piece of history about my current situation, other than it's part of some *deal.*

The High Lord stiffly moves on, our interactions almost a rehearsed dance at this point. "I have one more suitor lined up, from—"

"*No.*"

Azure eyes flash my way, his posture stiffening as his voice carries loudly in the room. "You scared the last suitor off with your petulant behavior," he complains through thin lips. "Talking of nothing but *donkeys* and how you are allergic to tomatoes."

"Donkeys are useful," I defend, trying desperately not to laugh. To his credit, it must be hard finding someone for me—I have a habit of being paired with a man and immediately discovering the best way to annoy him. The latest one loathed the sounds donkeys make, so I talked endlessly about them and how it's my dream to have one as a pet, especially since they're such efficient guards for livestock. The allergy bit was because he made fun of a woman allergic to cow's milk, and knowing that his lands are heavy producers of tomatoes, well, it would be quite annoying to have a wife with that affliction.

"He saw right through it and thought you were abhorrently mad."

"Honestly, not a bad assessment on his end," I mock, something invigorating me that used to lie dormant in fear. Maybe I've been struck one too many times. *Or I'm writing to someone who would happily break this entire castle, and honestly, I want to help, even if it collapses over my own body.* "I doubt I have any true sanity remaining after living like a caged bird, healing her broken bones and wounds."

He hotly moves away from his desk, fingers rolling like he's ready to hit me in our usual exchange of hatred. "You're so fucking useless. And have *no* idea the horrors you have avoided. You complain of being hit? We could so easily use sharpened steel. But we don't. All you do is complain about the luxury *forced* upon you, as you always say."

I grab my dress, holding it out as if it's a display. "What *luxury* is this? It's cold fabric that only offers warmth stolen from my own body—"

His voice is rapt with ire, and I dart my gaze to the floor, nostrils flaring since I know that look in his eyes, and I don't want to be hit *again*. "If you only knew the life you would have lived if it weren't for my wife! Any life as the wife to *any* lord is a luxury, you selfish cunt." He moves near, and I take a step back to the door, refusing to look up. "You ruin this last one, Victoria, and I will bind your hands in marriage to Lord Faust. He won't care that you're not willing. And I doubt he'll let you heal yourself as I do. He's made from the same fabric as the Unseelie, but I could absolutely use his army. The only reason I haven't chucked you at his feet is because Dahlia would have hated it, but I'm *this* close —" he nearly pinches his fingers together "—to not caring anymore."

My lips part, his words ice on my skin as I slowly raise my glare at Silas. "Faust is an old, disgusting man who would do *horrible* things to me. There's a reason she would hate to know I went to him."

His laugh is laced bitterly with rage, and I hate the shape of his teeth. "Better hope your next suitor likes you, then."

I almost call Silas a bastard, or throw a glare right into the eyes I despise the most. Instead, I quietly leave, just as he wants. Just as *I* want. My compliance has nothing to do with obedience. My deepest desire to flee is so loud that I'll play whatever part he needs, as long as it buys me his blind eye.

Because I'm done.

I *will* find a way out.

He says I can't leave his grounds, but would he follow me to Kane? Perhaps this is how the Unseelie High Lord collects his followers, humans and fae alike, who are worn down by a system so polluted with corruption that eating anything from its soil would be consuming poison. We flock to him. To a *new* life, no matter the cost.

No matter the damn cost.

If there's no letter when I get back, then I'm writing a new one.

Once I traverse the grand halls, pass the stained glass and climb an annoying number of stairs—panting heavily by the time I reach the top—I close the door to my tower suite and lock it, hurrying over to my table as if to prove to myself it's *not* all in my head, that escaping *isn't* futile. Underneath my blank parchment—an envelope.

No.

He wrote me?

Truly?

My pounding heart shifts in its rhythm as I stare at the sealed thing, the wax missing any emblem. It must have been delivered by Ginger while I was gone.

He wrote me again.

For a while, I simply stare until my eyes burn, not wanting to ruin such a moment. This could be the last correspondence I ever receive from Kane, meaning this opportunity I cling madly to will cease to end. Right now, it's a lending hand when I'm so tired of climbing my way out, but reaching up to take it could reveal the hand will forever disappear.

I don't want it to.

Once I can't stand the anticipation any longer, I open the letter that's made of lesser quality parchment, and something more than papyrus hits my senses.

I immediately smell *him*.

My eyes widen, his intoxicating musk so faint. It takes me back to when I saw him in person, his scent permeating the crowd. I assumed it was because of his rank, that perhaps the Unseelie simply had that effect on us Seelie, like a cat smelling out a dog. What would I do if he were in the room—

The thought flashes my eyes open, and I put the letter down so hastily it nearly slides off my desk.

What am I doing? Kane is an *Unseelie*. How can I be feeling anything more than animosity, or desperation to escape, toward him? The Unseelie want every last one of my kind dismantled and ripped from our homes. Including Kane. And I'm not daft. I know if he were to break out of the Carrows, he'd likely not take me. What am I going to do? Plead as I hold up these letters as if they will act as a shield?

He's *bored* in there.

My reality and deluded heart will not stop warring with each other, like two caged birds squawking about details that don't matter, because they're still locked behind bars, breathing in stale air rather than the petrichor.

And I don't even know him! Or, even worse, all I *do* know are the heinous rumors of what he does to his enemies. He carries a heavy reputation, and even *I* know not to make a deal with him I'm not willing to uphold. He *is* just like Faust in that manner.

Why did I even start writing to him in the first place?

But as I pull away, something snags my heart like barbed wire. I have to read the letter. I *must*. It's something I've started, and it's honestly the only thing in my life that gives me any anticipation I don't fear. Opening it up, the unfolding of paper so loud in a room that seems eternally quiet, even the faintest detail of knowing what his handwriting looks like does something to me.

Victoria,

I wonder if it's even worth telling you to stay away again.

Do you feel lost? Is that why you write me?

What do you hope to gain by contacting me? I am quite an unreachable man, and yet you have done so, even within these walls.

Perhaps you should question why an Unseelie like me would want to speak with the daughter of a Seelie High Lord. Why I ignore nearly all those who seek me out, but I spend the time to write you.

Tell me of your guesses, little flower.

I am not aware for how long I stare at this letter.

Many things course through my body, and yet I keep looking at *'little flower'*.

What does that mean?

Sliding into my chair to write him back, a thousand feelings collide in my chest in a complicated maelstrom, and I let my response flow freely, consequences be damned. Once finished, I fold the note and rub it along my neck—three times, for good measure. I know he must have done the same to his.

For what reason? I don't know.

I simply do not know.

And yet, I recklessly indulge before crying until the sun crests behind the trees to beckon the night.

Kane

Chapter 4

Drip.

Drip.

"Tell it to me again," I state, my cavernous cellar nearly pitch black. If it weren't for the morning sun that has yet to fully rise, not a shadow would exist. It would *all* be darkness.

Just as my instincts prefer it.

Osman leans his head down, our sight, as Unseelies, able to penetrate this darkness better than others, his eyes even slightly glowing like how an animal's might within a forest. *My* senses are even stronger.

How I grow tired of these walls.

"I know you are exchanging letters with *her*," he states, knowing not to say her name for her own protection. "So when I heard that Lord Faust is planning what I told you—"

"Repeat the exact words, Osman."

"Why does it matter?"

He lowers his head in submission when I glare at him without forgiveness—he will not disobey any orders related to her. I repeat, "Say it."

"Lord Faust is planning to buy Silas and his men. Through *her*. Through marriage."

The fucker called Faust has no idea who resides in Lady Victoria's shadows, and if he did, he'd wouldn't even *breathe* near her. Not once he knew the obligations I have to Victoria.

It's time to leave this place. Time for the world to be reminded of who I am.

ANOTHER NOTE IN ANOTHER BOOK, which lies on the tattered fabric of my bed. The little flower wrote back, despite the dangers.

How very good of her to write again. She is doing well, even if I question her judgment. She knows to answer the call of her mate, despite having no idea that's what's happening.

Kane,

Little flower is quite a unique name to call me... what does that mean?

Also, I am not sure why you write me. I am not sure why I write you. Perhaps you have a guess, instead?

If I were to proffer up one... I'd say it has something to do with wanting to strike at a weakness of my father's. Lull me into false security. Get me to reveal things I shouldn't. Otherwise, I can't imagine why out of all the people that want your attention, you'd give it to me.

Am I wrong?

Victoria

i.e., the little flower who is more astute than most give credence

I smile. I rather enjoy how pointless this dialogue is, in the grand scheme of things. She's completely wrong, as she has nothing to do with any of my political strategies.

This is entirely personal.

But she clearly doesn't understand the depth of what that means, so her assumptions are completely in line with logic. She's making the best observation that she can. Which is a reminder of how very little of the world she knows, and that patience will be needed as that glass cage is shattered—

I catch her scent, breathing it in like a starving creature who's finally aware of their stomach growling with avarice, the deep pangs of hunger from an unmated bond fully felt for the first time.

There's some kind of floral musk, something I have yet to smell in others. It's not flowery like roses, but its scent of nectar is one of the most pleasant things I have ever encountered. Those instincts scratch at me again, telling me she utterly belongs to me, and I to her. That I can, and should, have her body in every way she needs. Every way *I* need.

I glance down at the paper as I pull it from my face.

It's not too late.

I can burn this and never reply.

I should.

But she is alone in that castle, surrounded by strangers. By those she thinks she knows, including herself.

Rescuing her means I will *not* back away. If the scent of her letter drives me this mad, what would her actual presence do? I'd bite her pretty neck to leave my mark as soon as I could. Fuck her until I'm drained, then pet her hair as I breathe her in. Let no other male touch her until our bond is solidified. And then fill her again until she's leaking down her leg—

Fuck.

I can *feel* what even the *idea* of her does to me, my cock hardening like it's begging to be scented by its mate. She has no idea, I imagine, that there exists something between us. Something above and beyond the two of us. Something that grows more rare by the year, with wars eradicating mates before they ever meet.

Would I be too much for this false Seelie princess? Would she ever accept me for who I am? It's the only thought that makes me reconsider... but she knows of me and sent a letter. Even scenting it. She pines for me, whether she knows it or not.

No, I won't turn away. I will soothe that ache for her.

STEPPING out into the bitter morning air of the courtyard, the worn metal door slams shut behind me. The yard is bleak—no grass, rusting equipment, and shadows that stretch far too long for this time of day. The terrain provides *just* enough to train those who are eager.

Moving with deliberate steps as my boots crunch the hard-packed dirt beneath my feet, I always ensure those here know *this* space belongs to me when I occupy it. The *change* that's coming will not be weathered by grace or kind hearts; if I am to lead, I must wear a mask at all times. Those underneath me have all chosen a ruthless leader to follow, one who takes care of his own but doesn't hesitate to kill others. Even whole flocks of them at once.

I'll cull the weeds to protect the garden.

Eyes shift to stare once I'm through the threshold. Some are wary, while others feel the need to openly challenge, even if they won't get close, and others pretend not to notice me at all. The remaining half are devout followers who lower their heads in my direction. I don't acknowledge them, but I'm aware of who they are, and they know that.

Human men sit low on the crumbling steps, a few lifting weights, others murmuring amongst themselves. And then there are *them*—the Seelie males. Cleaner, sharper, with the cold arrogance of fae who believe their blood makes them untouchable, even in here.

They're clustered together near the pull-up bars, laughing too loudly, too performatively, when their attention turns to me. The air thickens with the musty scent of dominance and tension. *They* are the only ones I turn to face. There's no retreat within these walls, no one to hide behind other than themselves.

"Strange," one of the new Seelie shouts, voice smooth like glass. "I thought the High Lord's pet was supposed to be hiding in the shadows. Not strutting around like a wild dog."

Oh, his loyalty is placed within the wrong male. One of my greatest pleasures is watching all of the Seelie realize how much they've utterly failed. *This* is also the reason I operate the way I do—everyone always wants to fucking challenge who is in charge. I need to assert who I am among these people, and that being approached by me is something they should all *fear,* not desire. "We have a peacock living among us now, I see," I loudly say, sitting down on one of the worn benches with heavy weights next to it, before lifting my gaze to look at him.

He squares up, chest puffed and mouth cocked into a smirk. "You have a false sense of bravado in here, Kane." He gestures around. "You're *never* going to leave here. Can't exactly rule from these walls, can you? I heard you run this place as if you still *matter.*"

The motion to the yard stills, every man slowing in his rep to pause and watch what happens next. I could ignore this cunt. The time to leave is nearly imminent, and I'm not worried about the dichotomy shift here. But the sharp features of his cheeks are like a mockery of everything my people have suffered. It's this very arrogance from all the Seelies that makes them believe they're *superior.*

He's been sent to the Carrows, so that means the world would rather forget he exists.

His death would mean nothing.

I take a moment to stare at him before rising back to my feet, taking a few steps within this silence, catching a glimmer of concern in his annoyingly blue eyes. "And why are *you* here?" I ask.

"That doesn't matter."

I stop only once I'm within arm's reach of him,

aware of all who are present in this yard and that those loyal to me outnumber the rest. "Then neither do you."

The wrangle that follows is quick as I grasp the Seelie's throat, feeling the satin texture of his skin under my fingertips as they dig into him, closing off his airways. The sounds of gasps and muffled struggles fill the utter silence, accompanied by the sickening scent of iron from both of us—he claws at me, but I don't move, my arm completely flexed as I focus solely on this. Then, I smell the blood from his mouth. I witness the fear reflected in his widening eyes, a silent acknowledgment of realizing he will die, and it was so uncomfortably sudden, while none of the other Seelie come to defend him. Gradually, the resistance weakens, the spattering for air fading. His eyes lose their vitality, and I find peace knowing that one more pompous cunt is removed from this world that broke it in the first place.

Releasing my hold, his body collapses limply to the ground, a heavy thud echoing through the stillness as he sprawls on the ground with no fight. Casting a steely gaze at his companions, they freeze in apprehension. Blood drips down my arm and fingertips from where he clawed deeply, my skin burning, but it's a sensation that means little to me anymore. "Clean this mess, or the duskborns will. They don't like cleaning duties, so choose your battle wisely."

"*You* killed him. We shouldn't clean it up," a voice, brave and slightly trembling, sounds off from behind one of the Seelie.

"Theron, continue to cull them until they understand their place here," I say, giving them my back to return to my seat, lying down after gripping the weights to begin a long, arduous day of training to keep my body as capable as possible.

The sound of the Seelie males quickly changing their words to apology as I hear the many footsteps of my men approach them is the fuel I need. They're so afraid of what's coming, and they *should* be. Above, the sky is a bruised, grey canvas, heavy with the promise of rain. They'll quickly understand who reigns supreme in this shadowed place. Who *will* reign supreme over these lands.

As I focus on flexing and building my body, I move to the sound of another Seelie—sounds like the one who spoke out against me—screeching while he fights for his life, until the only sounds left are of someone dragging multiple bodies.

The ones that survive can live as prisoners in *my* new world.

And Victoria—thoughts of her almost derail everything within me, my awareness of the surrounding area vanishing almost instantly. No, I cannot let her go to another. Not now that I know she exists, and that she reaches out to me. I don't know what she'll think of this world I will create, but as long as her mate soothes her, she will learn to adapt.

Victoria

Chapter 5

Sheets soaked in sweat are what I awake to that morning, the fabric cooling when I reposition myself.

Sitting up to pull back the hair from my face, my hearth barely kindles to let in any light. Once on my feet, my night sweats mean nothing to me as I begin to freeze, wrapping my shivering body with a wool blanket as I stoke the fire.

It's my damn *heat*. It's been a week since I wrote Kane, and it's as if smelling his damn parchment made my body ignite. I told Ginger *no one* is to come near me, especially nothing from the Carrows. Not while like this.

The only blessing is that Silas stays so far away from me when this happens that it's like he never existed. It's just me and my shadow in here, with Ginger periodically making cold baths for my body to rest in. Riding out a heat alone is one of the cruelest jokes.

My gaze flits to my desk, knowing *his* letter is there. Yesterday was the first reprieve, and my anticipation for his words couldn't handle any more delay, especially when Ginger informed me that Kane wrote almost immediately. It did something to my soul to hear that, which unnerves me. It's why I didn't read it right away. I still haven't. It's just sitting on my desk, waiting to continue our conversation.

This night sweat is much less than the previous night, so I know by tomorrow I should feel closer to normal. It couldn't hurt to look now, right?

After adding another log onto the fire, I stare at the open letter I refused to look at as if the very act will take me away from here, like I'm terrified it will stop existing. What is it like to live outside the confines of Silas? To stoke a fire within walls much different than here?

To be free?

At least freer than I currently am… to find someone to ride out these heats with. To *choose* someone. Or no one. Maybe with each heat I'll fuck a different man.

Kane is using me, that's undeniable, but I can use him. I can try to dissect his words so I can manipulate him to let me out of here. I can serve as a healer, or *anything*.

My only hesitation as I stare at the piece of parchment is that its stagnation is one of the most comfortable things I've experienced in so very long, the pause in our communication waiting on *me* to write him back, instead of obsessing over when his reply will come.

I remind myself how grateful I need to be for this. At any moment, Silas could become aware. Waiting too long could ruin this small connection to the outside world.

Fuck it. I'll give Kane all of Silas's information if it gets me out of here. He can use me if I can use *him* for freedom. The unwritten unfolding of events only comforts me because I don't yet have to face failure, but I also *must* face reality. It's the only way out.

Once I pick it up, I hurriedly move next to the barely breathing fire for light, and I can't stop myself from immediately consuming his words:

Victoria,

That is not an unintelligible answer, but unfortunately, wrong. What I want from you is entirely selfish, I admit. So selfish, that I fear it too much for you. And yet, you cannot escape it, I do not think. You have been hidden from yourself for far too long, little flower.

What do you do in the castle all day? What men currently court you?

Kane

He signed his name.

Him.

And… entirely selfish? What does *that* mean?

It's as if I'm reading it like it's our first communication all over again. My body seems to forget how to function as everything is out of rhythm, especially as I bring the parchment to my nose and close my eyes when I *smell him*. What is happening to me? Why does this scent bring me a comfort that I never knew I craved? Is it my fading heat? Does it recognize the scent of a powerful fae? I put the letter down to bring clarity to mind, but I know I will pick it up to read it once more. Perhaps a hundred times, and each encounter will feel like the first.

What selfish motive of his? Isn't wanting Silas's information selfish? Too much of me? Does he not realize I'd give him the clothes off of Silas's back?

And yet, just when I think it will take me an entire day to formulate a reply, I find myself finishing it within only an hour, still by the fading firelight. Because I'm lonely, and bored. And needy. I wrap the letter in the nightgown I wore so it will be covered in me.

My heat.

I pause as I stare at what I penned him, almost disturbed at my action. The hells am I doing? He'll know it's my heat. He'll think I'm absolutely insane. *But I am, so what of it?*

I've always had a reckless side, but this feels manic.

Some part of my mind registers that we are sending

each other our scents, and that doing this might enrage him, even if I can't figure out why. Which means I absolutely commit to it, because someone at some point will get so mad at me they'll break these walls to get rid of me.

And everything in my bones screams to do so.

Kane

Chapter 6

Moonlight bathes over me as I stare at her letter in the solitude of my cell. Victoria's scent is noticeable even from a distance.

Why does it smell so much like her? As if... Blood sears my veins, all the way to my cock—when the parchment grazes the skin of my nose, even my lips, it's as if I can *feel* my pupils dilating.

Why did she do this?

It smells as if she just handed it to me rather than passed it through a chain of exchanging hands. I haven't smelled a single female's heat since being in here.

Everything ignites within my veins. Desire, lust, anger, infatuation, greed, possession, and *fear*. Did others smell this before reaching me? Is it stronger for me since she's *mine*? Do they keep her properly separated from any and all males? Tend to her to ease the lack of pair bonding?

"Little flower..."

I read the words very carefully, the concept of another touching her in such a state making me grind my jaw so tightly my teeth hurt.

Kane,

I am unsure how to respond about hearing this line of communication is purely selfish of you. Which only pushes me to consider the suspiciousness behind our exchange.

Nevertheless, it's more interesting than anything else I have at this castle. And the men in my life? Currently, there are none. Although, I suppose that answer shall mean very little, soon. I have a feeling my hand will be forced into marriage, even if they have to put me under a drugged spell.

And what do I do in the castle? I have a very tight schedule. I train with combat four mornings in a row and take three mornings off, as all members of our rank are required to do. I eat. And then I paint. A proper lady should paint, should she not?

I don't care much for the proper things. As indicated by wanting to write to you.

I wish to spend time in the woods. To be with animals. I am very happy among the wildlife. And not while wearing a pretty dress and singing to birds. I don't mind the dirt. I enjoy the moon and the crystals that shine in its light, but I don't think I am supposed to admit that. The moon is for the Unseelie and the duskborn, whereas the sun is for the Seelie. So this is akin to the moon writing the sun, isn't it?

I'd like a pet, I think. Something with no motive other than food and friendship. Something that can't break my heart.

What do you do in the Carrows, other than wait for me to write a letter?

Victoria

I breathe heavier. My little flower wrote to me with such conversation that so many possibilities seem to open all at once, and even threw a slight jab at me. With the ghost of a very faint smile on my lips, I stare out the window into the darkness of night, reviewing any and all undertones, smirking at the last question as I replay it.

She has a sassy side.

It truly does seem as if Silas plans to marry her off, one way or another. Rage fills me in ways where, for the first time, I *feel* the confines of this prison.

I don't burn this letter. If anything, I keep that scent under my pillow and risk it.

I need it.

TWO DAYS PASS BEFORE I write Victoria another letter, a series of events occurring before then that put every-thing into motion. There are many in here who are waiting to be bought like cattle. What would they do for me if I freed them? And just how many would be willing to cut off Silas's head while I string up his corpse over his castle's doors to let them know what happens when anyone even *hints* at coming near my mate?

It's time to see how they will act.

I can't help but wonder how much Victoria thinks of me in the absence of a letter, knowing that very soon she will be greeted by *me*, not the lady's maid who hands this to her.

When I finish writing her that night and hand it off, Osman comes to me, his usual poise slightly broken as he pants, "There's a riot."

Victoria

Chapter 7

Standing in the threshold of the castle, I'm allowed to wear pants today, even if I'm not training.

Shouldering my healer's bag, I'm heading to the Carrows, where an insurrection from a faction *not* belonging to Kane resulted in the duskborn being used to control the crowd. I heard Kane had sat back, watching. Waiting. Observing. Until the entire place broke out in a battleground and he killed over thirty prisoners and even a few duskborn, single-handedly.

A very firm reminder that this is *not* an ordinary fae. His unofficial claim as the leader of the entirety of the Unseelie is for a reason. What's said to have stopped him was a duskborn using a dagger laced with grimroot to subdue him. An option that will result in his fatality if left untreated.

To say I panicked when first hearing this news is an understatement.

Silas struts toward me underneath the heavy clouds that hang low like most days of the week, his judgmental eyes two things I abhor in this world. "You will heal him, and if lucky, return."

Hesitation binds my tongue until I can't help but ask, "I know you don't care for me, but my hand in marriage is something you prize. Why risk my life when you need my beating heart and womb to sell off?" If some aspect of survival wasn't speaking, I'd be as silent as the clouds that cast their shadows above. But I can't. This is just too bizarre. He even allowed me my healing pendant, which is currently tucked underneath my tunic as it hangs around my neck.

Usually, it's locked away in his stupid room where I'm only granted access when necessary.

"You complain endlessly of your marriage proposals," he remarks, taking a step forward, his hands clasped behind his back, the crowd of his armada giving us space to speak. "If you come back, you may come back *compliant*. If you do not wish to obey, then you remain."

My eyes widen, my nostrils flaring.

I understand now.

"You're effectively imprisoning me there," I mutter, my mouth so dry it's as if I chewed on cotton. "At the Carrows."

His grin is wicked. "Poor Kane is growing unruly in

there, and thought a fight might free him. He will *never* leave, and I need him alive to keep the Unseelie controlled. Strip away their leader, and then I have to figure out who the *next* one is before culling *him*. So, go. Heal the man you obsess over so his men can then defile you after—*yes*, I know you write him. I know you're probably obsessed because of what he did to Lawrence. It doesn't mean anything to me. With him in the Carrows, you might as well be writing a *ghost*.

"I'm showing you what prison is *truly* like. What a ruthless leader *really* is. He slaughtered thirty prisoners in there, all because a fight broke out, and he was killing all those associated, like a common beast claiming its territory. So enjoy being near *that* monster of a creature." A revolting pleasure floods his gaze. "And if you're idiotic enough to remain, then there is no hope for you as an ordained wife of a High Lord. I won't even risk it with Faust, who might just end up killing you before you're useful. Only you going to him compliant will help me."

My heart pounds so hard I can hear it in my ears, my head growing dizzy. Glancing down, I try to examine the way Silas's eyes glint with victory, and that he knew of me writing Kane this entire time. "But Kane," I question. His name on my tongue is like revealing a secret so tightly guarded I suddenly feel naked. "You want me to heal *Kane*. You said you think I'm writing him letters, and now you want me to heal him?"

Gods it's disgusting how he looks at me, like a

starving wolf that's finally cornered its prey so perfectly, as if I'll cut my own leg off to feed it to him. "You believe yourself to be such a victim, Victoria. Him scarring Lawrence was not for your benefit, Kane was asserting himself to *my* court, and for whatever reason, he thinks being in the Carrows sends a preferable message. It keeps him out of the world, so I don't care why he wants to be in there. He's *never* leaving. He *will* break you when you're no longer a benefit to me. And he *will* be healed, either by you or others. I know he's trying to get to me, through you. And in the same stroke, I show myself as a caring High Lord, even to his prisoners. Even to the *Unseelie*. Sending in his own adoptive *daughter*. Perhaps it will quell the noise of further insurrection." He leans in so far his breath is on my ear, and he smells of lemons. I nearly push him away, but the idea of him knowing he got to me is almost worse. "You will come back broken so I can use you without listening to your groveling, and Faust will be grateful to have you so shattered you'll be *happy* to see him at your marriage ceremony. I am done with this version of you."

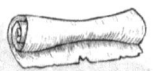

It took the entire ride on horseback down to the docks for me to process the conversation, even as we board the ship that will get us there, seagulls yapping in the air. My hand never quite leaves my healing pendant. It's so foreign to have it as if I own it. *I do own it. It's literally made with my blood.*

What if this all works in Silas's favor? What if Kane *has* been using me, and now he gets to mold me? Will he laugh maniacally when he sees what Silas has done? Like I'm the small rabbit that two wolves are toying with? Turn me into a weapon to use against Silas? Or just kill me and get me out of the way?

While making Silas look *noble* for healing his enemies...

Do I still have to heal Kane? I have to, right? Letting him die would leave me to the fate of his men. It was entertaining interacting with him from the safety of written word on paper, but even *I* have heard how brutal it is to be among Kane, and I live in a tower. Now that I see the dark, imposing walls of the Carrows on their own island in the distance, I'm struck with *fear*.

I sent that man letters with my scent all over them.

Despite the cold winds, my cheeks feel like they're on fire.

The prison island is larger than I thought, looming over us like a mountain among violent tides, windows carved out of the rock as if the oceans sprouted out a prison. The ship I sail on to reach the island pulls into a carved-out levee, the waters rising until we meet land. It's all entirely cold and made of the same gray stone, my nose numb in the frigid air. I keep tucking loose strands of black hair behind my ears, although I suppose worrying about my appearance is the least appropriate thing right now.

The monotonous grey of the Carrows is loud against the vibrancy of Silas's castle.

A true prison.

There's an undeniable elegance in this monstrosity that all the Seelie courts send their unwanted prisoners, and yet it's completely worn down with time and misery. After crossing through the courtyard, the double doors open like an opening to a void. Walking through the front entry, there's a moisture in the air from the drizzling rain, one that makes everything about this place that much more miserable.

My eyes seem to adjust quicker than the rest, spotting a few duskborn near a corner, lingering just beyond the reach of the light. Silent. Watchful. As we make our way through, I notice some sit like gargoyles with gleaming eyes. Not with madness. No, that would be too typical of stories we tell children. This is calculation. Recognition. A knowingness that makes my skin itch, like they're aware I come from the place they serve, and *loathe*. It's hard to peel my eyes away when I hear about them all the time, the creatures bred by the Seelies to hunt down the Unseelie in their own land.

They're so *tall* and thick with muscle, their silvery hair almost silken. Their angles are sharper, and so are their fangs. Their breed is said to be bred and born all in complete darkness within the systems of caves that require blood offerings from the Seelie. The ones at the Carrows are bred in the very caverns of this place, taking advantage of their fiercely protective nature over their homeland.

Perfect guards that can catch any escapee.

If any part of this goes poorly, I'm truly and dearly fucked.

So why does that not terrify me?

We advance deeper into this place, guided by a Seelie guard, my wool cloak still covered in small droplets of water. Even the wax of the candles is made with a darker color. It's so quiet that our footsteps echo throughout until I can hear the clamor of inmates.

Focus.

It's *their* presence that makes me anxious. The idea that I survived Silas all these years, only to meet my death at the hands of people inside of here that spins so much bitter resentment in my stomach.

What am I to do here? Heal Kane and leave to see who my next suitor is before Faust gets hold of me? It seems like Silas doesn't trust me with the next suitor and is skipping right to the twisted one. And yet, I already know my answer. Kane wants me for one reason or another, but if he can secure my freedom, I don't care what I have to do.

Lean into that.

We may have had a momentary sense of fun, but giving him my concern seems entirely unwarranted. It's no longer something to get me through the days. Interacting with him will break any illusion of safety I had, and if Silas is telling the truth, then I need to be as cunning as all these puppeteers who think I'm still affixed to strings.

The corridor narrows, stone arching overhead like a closing throat. Iron sconces flicker low with golden flames, casting shadows that crawl and slither along the walls like they know I shouldn't be here. The further I walk, the more the air thickens. Not just with cold, but with... *presence.*

I start to feel it before I see them—his people.

Can I *sense* the Unseelie?

The prison has many cells, some of which are large and dark, with people chained to corners. Then there are those that are isolated, but still held behind iron bars. Some only have doors, and sometimes I even see the cells that are wooden coverings in a hole in the floor.

When we pass a particularly large collection of people who are all living within the same confined space, one of them leans slightly forward, a grin spreading far too slowly across his face. His teeth are bloodstained, and he *sniffs* the air. "She smells like warmth," he murmurs to no one, to everyone. "That won't last."

I don't flinch. I *won't.*

Another one, massive and tattooed, slams a fist against the bars, the metal ringing out like a funeral bell. "Oh, we'll *eat* that softness right off your bones."

The guard that guides me stiffens but keeps walking.

And it's the way none of them seem shocked that gives me deep worry. It feels orchestrated.

Like I'm being escorted as a sacrifice to the altar.

The only thing I can't control is my rapid breathing, something I hope is well hidden behind a stolid visage.

The only bit of sanity remaining is when we pass a giant archway that reveals the library I've heard so many stories of. So far, it's the only place that's offered any natural light. Being greeted by the sun after passing through such darkness is, admittedly, a humbling experience.

It doesn't last for long as we round another corner, the sunlight even more prominent through aged, foggy windows that reveal a massive courtyard where people are training and fighting. "Do *those* men have better behavior?" I ask, the sunlight almost like protection, giving me a semblance of calm.

"I wouldn't assume that at all," the guard says. "The one who offered to eat your flesh had just come in from the courtyard."

"Oh."

Okay, so not a single inch of this place is to be trusted.

The narrow tunnels consume us once more until dumping us out into a mezzanine with a large, circular hole in the ceiling for sunlight, a built-in dirty pond below where water drips down.

It's *then* that I catch the faintest scent of Kane, so

small it's like passing a vase of fresh flowers, but I'm not sure where it comes from.

On the lower level exists multiple hallways, and it's when we approach one in particular that we're finally met with the greeting of another fae with short hair and a scar so deep it looks like a stone carver missed and gouged a chunk out. His eyes widen, just for a breath, as they meet mine. Probably wasn't expecting *me*. Every bit of my bones screams so loudly that I need to get out of here, and yet, when I glance over my shoulder, some of the prisoners are watching. And the duskborn now stand in the entry that we used to get here.

Oh, I don't like this. I don't like the sensation of being forced in here.

Prison.

"*You're* the healer they sent?" His voice is all gravel and disbelief. Not mocking, but close. "I thought…" he looks at the guard that guided me. "I thought when some spotted the High Lord's ship with a healing flag it was a rumor."

"Turns out to be true," the guard replies.

"He sent his *daughter*?"

"Adopted," I clarify, although the glare from both men makes me think that's not politically relevant. "He wants me to heal Kane." I manage out. "As an offering of good faith, I believe."

I owe Silas no loyalty here, but I'm not admitting I'm being sent here as punishment.

Both men laugh, the corners of their mouths

stretching up before shaking their heads. "What kind of good faith matters in this shit hole?"

My body hollows out, although this isn't entirely too unfamiliar. I've been laughed at before by Silas's men. "Do you want him healed or not?" I press.

The man looks me over again, more carefully this time. Not like he's assessing strength, but potential collateral. Concern flickers in his eyes, followed quickly by hesitation—and something else. Pity, maybe. Or regret. Until the guard that guided us loses patience and grabs my shoulder to shove me forward.

I nearly stumble, and do my best to catch my composure. The scarred man says, "He has been poisoned. A blade was used that had been laced with black magic, something to slow the spread to make it worse."

"There's not a single healer here?" I ask.

"No." There's no explanation needed.

Well, so far, it seems like Silas really has just sent me to the Carrows. Which means the next interaction with Kane will likely seal my fate. The hallway isn't long, and leads to a singular door where the man nods to it as if to apologize for my fate. I breathe slowly, my hand slightly shaking as I grip the door handle. The scent of Kane is so strong I hesitate, just standing there like a statue, my satchel sliding forward so I have to catch it.

I'm so fucking nervous to be alone with him. Especially after the stupid letters and *scenting* them. The last two years of obsession might as well have only been a week, and they feel so *wasted*. All culminating to now, and I know this won't be pretty.

Get this over with.

When I open the door and step inside, the door shuts behind me with the finality of a grave. Iron grinding against iron in a locking mechanism that nearly vibrates in my teeth. If I weren't so distracted by the massive man on the cot, I'd pay more attention to how dramatically my chest rises and falls.

Muscle is corded tight under torn skin, his torso barely covered with ragged edges of what used to be a shirt. Blood is crusted around a long, jagged wound on his stomach that pulses with something too dark to be just an infection.

But it's his *stillness* that makes it worse.

He's not unconscious.

He's waiting.

The room reeks of him in fantastic ways. There's also an undertone of power, something that Silas resonates: *a High Lord.* His hard, steel eyes are wide, burning right through me as he slowly inhales.

Even in pain, even drugged, there's a tension to his body like a beast at the edge of lashing out. Kane grimaces when he tries to rise, placing a hand on his gut where his blood reeks of poison. "Why're you here?" he manages out, his grumbling voice sending shivers down my back. His broad jaw is so tight he looks like he may bite—and yet, there's the smallest part of me that is wholly unafraid.

72

A dark, magnetic pull wraps around my spine and tugs, something entirely ancient. The kind of scent that lives in old instincts. I don't even know what that means, but it's what I feel.

To my greatest surprise, the primary emotion I feel is *disappointment*. Everything about his body language reeks of frustration, rather than intrigue. It reminds me that not long ago, that ruthless gaze had just witnessed the murder of many, caused by his very own hands. Some of the blood smeared on him might not even be his.

Broad, veined hands move to position himself, the muscles from his lower stomach to his shoulders all moving and flexing. *Gods* he is powerful, even in here. What does he look like when his training is unrestrained?

"Why're you *here*?" His voice is low. Rough. A scrape of sound that isn't amused—it's *knowing*. It's as if the magic eating through his veins is just a passing nuisance. Like *I'm* the one in danger.

And maybe I am.

No, I definitely am. I can't even smell the guard anymore. They left me here. "I'm a healer, if you didn't know." My voice sounds too sure, too sharp—like something brittle trying to hold its shape under weight.

I fidget with my bag as I place it on the floor, gathering a few supplies when I refuse to let him get to me. Out of my peripheral, I notice that when he's not boring his gaze into me, he's watching the door, as if ready to barricade it.

All the while, the chill of this place clings to my skin.

Even though I have a task at hand, it feels as if there are leagues between us in this rather small room. "I know this is all odd, considering that Silas imprisoned you. But he loathes me and wants me broken for Faust. To be frank, healing you would bring me great joy just to make Silas angry. So I will do so to my best capability."

His lips twitch—like a man trying not to sneer. Or speak. Or growl. His broad shoulders are hunched slightly as if he'll spring into action.

Duty and obligation push me forward, while self-preservation whispers words of caution. "I'll begin to heal you, then."

My own voice sounds far away. I don't wait for permission. There isn't any, not really. What other options are there? I'm imprisoned in my own rights with Silas, so it's not as if happiness will appear on its own. Leaving him will require incredible sacrifice.

But perhaps, for now, I can be of use to Kane. Even just as a healer. Even if that's all I'll ever be.

I eye his stomach once more as I near him. Bright red blood now oozes with the black toxins polluting him. "I am going to heal the wounds. This may take a while."

He doesn't answer. Just *stares*. I kneel to examine where he was stabbed in the stomach, reaching into my canvas bag to acquire the necessary bandages, ointments, and a bowl. When I glance up, his gaze is pinned on me—unblinking, unreadable. Like he's trying to memorize the shape of me in case I vanish. Or betray him.

Of course, I lower my gaze immediately. I have absolutely no idea how to read this man. The silence grows as our tension thickens, and for a moment, I feel like an idiot as I swear Silas's words are about to ring true.

My fingers brush the hilt of the dagger I brought with me—just in case. My hand lingers a breath too long. Kane notices. Of course he does.

But he still doesn't move.

Heal the bastard. Removing my necklace, I wrap the chain around my hand so the pendant hovers at my palm. I immediately begin to work, slathering a green-tinted balm that will numb his skin on his wound before hovering the very hand with the pendant over it, concentrating deeply on pulling the poison out as if my hand were a magnet and the toxins a metal. It will be painful. The pendant presses against my palm rather than dangle—a sign my magic still works, a reminder that there's *something* Silas can't take from me. The tips of my fingers radiate a pale glow as my ability to heal is enhanced. Some say that those like me, if trained under magnificent legends, can even bring beating hearts back from the dead as long as it's been less than a moon's cycle.

I mostly take care of the superficial things, as that's

all I've ever been taught to do—black sludge leaks out, sliding against his skin that's warm in color, even in here. Slightly darker than my own. Kane stiffens immensely, inhaling deeply through his nostrils.

"What is the pain level?" I ask, breathing deeply to catch the scent of how much this ravages him. I can always smell the damage more than I can see it.

"It's manageable," he grinds out.

I reach into my bag to retrieve fresh linen and a jar filled with a thick ointment of bitterroot and fermented myrah, which is used specifically for this affliction. "You stiffened quite a lot for it to be manageable."

"It's not from the pain." A large clot of poison slumps out into my bowl, disintegrating into liquid once my hand, which hovered over to extract it, is no longer pouring magic into it. "This is no place for you. This—" He stops abruptly, looking around as if this is the most annoying thing he's encountered lately. "Someone was coming to heal, to bring me what I needed *aside* from an antidote. *You* are not supposed to be here."

Suddenly, I feel rather vulnerable, small. I stare at the massive, flat plane of his abdomen where blood and toxin still ooze, aware of how I'd have to crane my head just to look him in the eyes. "Every second matters, so I'm not going to stop, even if this is no place for me," I say, purposefully not looking up. I will prove Silas so wrong that he'll grovel on his knees. If I *am* to die here, it will be because *I* allow it.

I'm *not* going back to that fucking castle.

The only movement is his steady breathing. The curious fog my mind found within dissipates, no longer lost in a fantasy of whatever the letters were.

I recite a few words until my fingertips tingle with magic while I continue to pull it out of him. I maintain not looking up at him as I channel my energy to focus on the rot of this poison, feeling its foreign vibrations underneath his skin as I guide it to the torn tissue with the unnatural opening. I move my hands along him, his wound opening slightly as more black sludge bubbles out. With my other, I catch it in the same bowl to examine and confirm the poison with a few droplets of various ingredients I brought, inspecting to see if he should require a more complex antidote.

For some reason, as I do this, I *need* to look up, and when I do…

He's already intently staring.

Gods does that gaze unwind me. Those silver eyes are like metal, sharp and dangerous. In this darkness, lit only by a few candles, that face appears even more rugged, with a shadow of facial hair, one that mirrors the scalp of his head. A scar runs from his jaw to his temple, while another slashes through his eyebrow, his bottom lip scarred just the same. And from this angle, he appears even *more* massive.

"This is beyond reckless," he states, judgment heavy in his gaze. Not angry. Not grateful. Just—*watching*. Absorbing.

"It's either this or I get to marry Lord Faust, and I'd

rather face this place than belong to him for the rest of my life." It's not my particular desire to speak of such drama, the sound of it so meaningless in a purposeless place such as this.

"No, you wouldn't have," he replies through steady breaths. "Faust would have been drawn and quartered the moment I got out of here."

That metallic gaze bores into me like hot iron, and yet it doesn't feel like a predator sizing up prey. It feels like something dangerous in a different way—like he's memorizing the shape of my soul. It's so much that I feel the need to utterly flee.

"Many of those prisoners—" he takes in a sharp breath as another large clot slides out into the bowl "—would risk losing *limbs* to fuck you until you can't move. That's hardly the worst of what they'd do to you."

I nearly choke on my spit, not ready for such bluntness. "Do you want me to heal you or not?" I quip with an annoyingly high-pitched voice, staring him down as I meet that liquid gaze.

"*Victoria.*"

My name on his tongue is so... no. Him using my name shouldn't have such a powerful command on me.

"*Kane.*"

His eyes flash with an intensity that annoyingly frightens me, and I begin to accept that the letters— whatever their purpose—were *not* an invitation. Do people even call him by his name? Did I just cross a serious line? "I have not secured myself here, yet. That was to come with liberation. This is risking your life."

I don't know what to do with that statement, or those undertones. I refocus. "Well, Silas ordered me here. I don't want to go back. At all. So this is what it is."

"Oh, you're *not* going back."

If the lighting were better, I might be able to understand why I swear his face displays pride, greed, and rage all at once. A part of my mind spins the longer he stares at me, his scent thickens with the masculine stains, and somehow it's completely comforting.

"Do you know what *we* are?" he asks.

I hate that my gaze is pulled, no *dragged*, to his lips, especially the scar that cleaves through. *Perhaps magic is at play. Contorting my logic.*

"Maybe you can enlighten me," I defensively reply.

Kane leans down over me, slowly crowding the space between us, his thick thigh now shifted so I'm in between both legs while I remain kneeling. My hatred for Silas locks me into this position, refusing to back away as it feels like I can't swallow the knot in my throat. I prepare for so many things to happen...

His breathing mixes with a low, guttural sound that could only be described as a growl, my gaze locked onto his stomach that slightly bleeds from the movement as he speaks from above me. "I have half a mind to cover you entirely with my scent, so it's impossible to mistake who has made a claim on you."

The words singe my mind like an oil fire.

It's *then* that I scramble to my feet, having no idea what to make of that statement. Blood rushes to my feet as I place the wall to my back, reaching for the door handle only to find it's locked. "Is *that* the purpose of writing to me? To bring me here and defile me?"

"I tried to stop you," he begins, making no effort to stand or chase me in this small room. There's no need, I'm at his utter mercy no matter where I am in here. "It's my duty to soothe your agitation." His steel gaze lowers to look over my body. "*All* of your agitation… as your mate."

His words sink into my brain, which sears hot at the revelation. *Mate…* I press as firmly as possible against the cold wall. "Absolutely not."

He remains where he's at, his gaze darkening like a predator that's confirmed it *will* have its prey. "Why, little flower?"

I swallow thickly, the dark room like a cage. Pieces of me scream with affirmation, their cries striking harshly against the fear that he's *right*. I'm nowhere near prepared for this. "Perhaps I have gone mad."

He leans forward from his sitting position, the room still smelling of the poison, but it no longer emanates from him—his scent is purely *him* now. "You couldn't stop writing to me because of our connection. Of the draw. You were desperate, and your soul reached out to the one resource that would do everything in his power to keep you safe. I told you not to write me, or else fate would seal itself. And I'm a man who would kill even the innocent to protect what's his, and your soul knows that. Somewhere in there."

Because either I am neglected or insane, I indulge in the *sensation* that those words elicit. It would explain so much, and I can't stop hearing the scratch marks those words are leaving on my soul—this is my way out.

Stop it. I must be neglected. A fated mate means leaving my current prison to accept the cuffs of another. I'm seriously supposed to bend to the idea that our souls are bound? That fate, some cruel magic, or the gods themselves have decided my worth and handed it over to him?

This is the same painting from Silas, just with different brush strokes…

Kane finally stands, and the shift in energy is immediate. My nostrils flare when I realize, despite my height, even with every inch of defiance in my spine, he is *much* larger than me. Worn boots move over the stone, his scent invading the space around me until there's nothing else to breathe. "I know you're aware of that, somewhere deep down. Why else write to me?"

I don't answer.

Stand tall, Victoria. This might be some of your last moments. Even if you're broken, stand for yourself.

Kane only seems enthralled, greed staining his silver eyes. Blood pounds in my neck when he reaches out to touch my throat with his rough hand. His fingers rest on the pulse hammering beneath my skin, and he *smiles*, just barely, like it answers a question for him. "And I admit, selfishly, that I want to mold you to me—" his fingertips move to the nape of my neck, gripping my hair, tightening as possession glints in his eyes like metal catching sunlight "—Have you ever been with a man?"

"No," I say, resolute.

Something flares in him. Not surprise. Not mockery. Just something *dark*, reverent. Like he's just been handed something priceless. "Then *all* of you will mold to me."

Wetting my lips, my dignity demands I at least *try* to fight whatever madness infects me. "That's bold of you."

"So was sending all those letters in violet ink, *covered* in your heat."

My knees don't buckle, but they *want* to. My lungs fight for breath. And all I can do is stare at him and *feel* —all the warmth, the fear, the treacherous ache coiled low in my belly. "What if I say no?"

This is not about romance. It's about *possession*. About identity. About the terrifying possibility that some part of me *wants* to belong to someone, especially if it means his care for me is his priority, if for anything else, because their very instincts will demand it.

"You cannot say I didn't tell you to stop, because now it's too late. I know what your hair feels like between my fingers, and how you smell when it's only our scent in the room." His gaze is feral, even if the rest of him seems controlled. "Even if you leave, I'll skin anyone who ever tries to touch you. The precious High Lord has no idea what he's just done."

A brittle laugh escapes over a cotton tongue. "You can't just say that and expect me to play along. I don't want to live that life anymore."

"I don't expect you to play *anything*," he says, close enough that I can feel the heat of his body, smell the iron tang of blood still clinging to him. "But you need to understand what you are to me. I wish I could pretend you were nothing," he says, voice so low it feels like it scrapes my skin raw. "I'd have an easier time letting you go, because coming to *my* world will be nothing short of catastrophic for your reality."

The sheer absurdity of how my body bends to every word that comes from his imperfectly perfect lips gives me the most hesitation. Even if there wasn't some *clear* hormonal shift at play, I'm too aware of my damaged heart. "I'm not in my right mind."

"Obviously," he retorts, a tempered ache bleeding through his gaze. "And neither am I... but here we are. And we *do* have a problem. You leave out this door without being covered in me, or my bite in your neck, and they'll rip you apart, especially with your scent of arousal that you can't hide, as *yes*, I can smell that. If I claim you, they'll think twice before touching you, and that will get you out of here alive."

By the gods, does my body demand I listen to him.

In fact, it's as if I'm feverish.

Shivers quake through me like nothing ever has

before. "I said no," I reiterate, every nerve in my body burning with defiance at those words.

Logic and this fever heat mix like oil and water, the desire for Kane mounting with each moment. All I want to do is consume, and have him consume me.

"What do you actually want from me?" I grind out. "I may have been locked in the tower for most of my life, but I'm past the naivety of a young girl. There's *always* a catch."

There's a pause, and within it, I can almost sense he might actually wish to guard this part of him. His grip on my hair tightens as he says, "I have suffered and sacrificed my entire life. The selfish side of me wants to enjoy the affection that this bond will offer."

Our bond. This thing that apparently exists without my permission, just like the rest of my life. I recognize the absurdity here, I know he's not wrong—having his scent all over me would act as the perfect shroud. "Why would those people out there kill me if Silas hasn't properly disowned me?"

"He has already done so by sending you here."

That cuts much deeper than I ever care to admit, my gaze dropping down to stare at his chest. At skin and muscles that belong to a stranger, and yet I can't deny that I'm pulled to him by more than just curiosity. "I don't really have an option, do I?"

"You do, just with one caveat," he drawls out, slightly pulling my head back to *hint* at the power he could exert over me. That display of dominance doesn't last as that intensity dissipates, something gentle burning away at the ferocity. "I'll give you the forests you asked for, and all the creatures to befriend, and tear down the walls that confine you, little flower. You will never return to anyone, but know if you don't come to me, I won't be able to leave you be."

The tension in my body loosens as I slightly lean forward, a slave to his words and promises. He's *mine* to enjoy, to touch and taste as I wish. If he's somehow my mate, then… maybe…

His eyes flash wide with concern, and he repositions us so I'm behind him as the door unlocks, the man from earlier entering. "*They've* arrived."

Kane slowly looks down at me, perhaps with even a trace of concern.

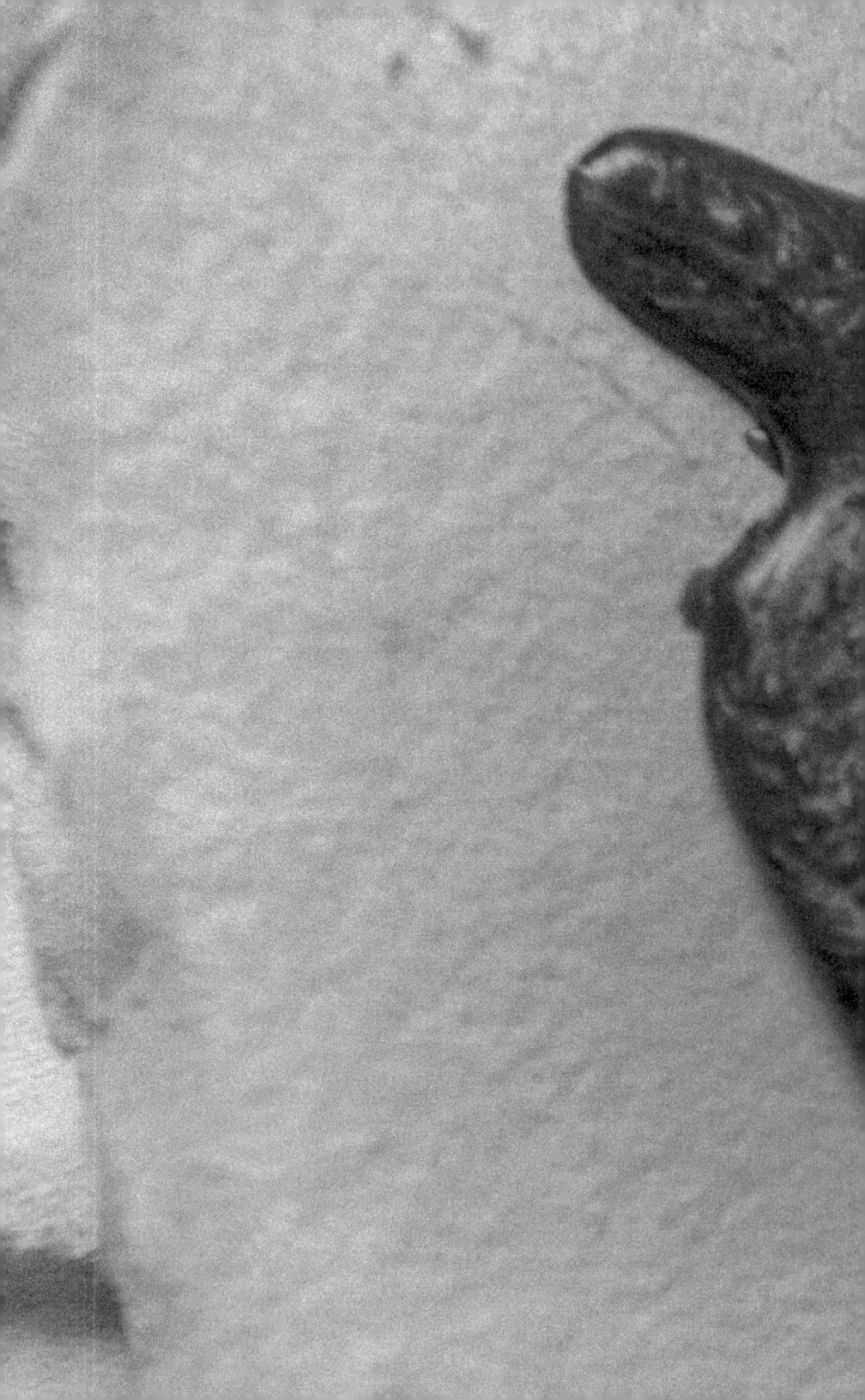

Victoria

Chapter 7

My stare is blank for longer than I'd like. It's such an impossible suggestion. It's not often my mind doesn't work like how I want it to, everything overwhelming common sense when a desire to run overwhelms me as I shove at his chest, which might as well amount to pressing against a stone wall. He catches my wrists mid-flight and presses me against the cold, unforgiving wall. His hands are iron shackles around my bones. The small bit of true force he just used is a massive indicator that as long as he's within arm's reach, I'm going nowhere. He lowers his face into mine. "You have no idea the trouble you're in by being here, Victoria. Do *not* take off."

Oh that comment pisses me off, my inner battle for decorum forced upon my life clashes with the side of me that's ready to *fly*. "My life is *nothing but* trouble," I snap, my voice splintering. "I don't want to hear about having it good. Just because my cage was gilded, doesn't mean I still wasn't in a *cage*. Why does *no one* understand that?"

His gaze drags over me, slow and assessing, like he's deciding exactly how broken I already am. "You are the daughter—adopted or not—of the man every Unseelie in here would love to see gutted and strung up like a pig. Only the Seelies would spare you, and there aren't many of them here."

"And what then?" I rasp, sagging against the wall. "What do I do, huh? I've been trying to figure out how to escape Silas for the latter half of my life, but it's not as if it's *easy*."

"You will stay very close to me," he states. "If it comes to it, I'll bite your neck first, but you're leaving this place untouched, unless by *me*. One way or another. Silas failed you miserably there, but I won't."

Those words are akin to gently stroking my hair while taking a perfectly warm bath, icing an ache so deep inside of me I don't know if I've ever been truly treated right. "That starts the mating bond," I reply, some part of my brain trying not to be *too* desperate.

He smiles. "And I plan to finish it. *Preferably* out of the Carrows, for your own dignity."

He actually believes we're mates. He smells divine, sure, but that could just be the lonely, neglected part of me steering. But I know Kane's knowledge of the world is beyond mine, so I can trust he wouldn't suggest this unless he was certain, right?

His voice sinks low, intimate and lethal. "We're leaving this room. There's a female among my ranks, Freya. If—*if*—I ever have to leave you alone, it'll only be with her."

I lift only my gaze, glaring at him through my lashes. "We're actually leaving? As in departing from the Carrows?"

He arches a brow. "The purpose for me being here has been served, and I want out of this shit hole as fast as possible. This attack was calculated, and it's time to leave, now."

He directs me with a nod to the door, his eyes hardening like Silas's would when entering the public. He leads the way into the cool, fetid air of the hall, positioning himself in front of me as the other man just assumes the position behind. We walk down the corridor, Kane moving with the presence of a man who doesn't need to shout to own a room. The sneers from the other Unseelie feel like a distant, feral cousin's greeting.

Nearing a larger door, we step into a wide room overflowing with more Unseelie, their few specks of weapons or armor catching the dim light like oil slicks against the few candles that are lit. Every head turns to judge me.

A woman approaches Kane as soon as we're through the threshold, sharp-eyed and thin-lipped. Her dark blonde hair cut evenly at her shoulders and to form bangs. My eyes widen as no one I know has hair remotely like this. "My liege, Mockingbird is underway."

Kane makes a sound of acknowledgement, looks off as if making a swift, final decision. "We need to speak in private, then," he replies, cold and final.

Without a word, the room empties—chairs scraping, boots pounding, mutters dying to silence. Only the woman remains, her gaze flicking to me with open suspicion. Even the man who was walking behind me gave us privacy as he shut the door. "Why is *she* here?" the woman asks, careful but probing.

Kane slightly turns to face me, looking me over with heavy consideration. The silence grows thick enough to choke on until he replies, "Because she's mine."

Every hair on my body rises, gooseflesh rolling out like I've been drenched in something beyond my understanding. The woman blinks, but wisely keeps her mouth shut.

He squares his shoulders. "Victoria is *never to* be left alone, and will be beside me unless I'm pulled elsewhere, to which you will guard her. Which is unfortunately right now, as I need to see to something without anyone nearby. No one comes in here."

Freya hesitates with a bobbing throat, not daring to glance up at him. "She belongs to Silas, sir."

Kane's eyes flash with a dangerous glint. "I know this is not what's expected, but if anyone ever says she belongs to him again, I will cut their tongue out." Both Freya's and my eyes widened. "The sooner it's understood that hurting her is akin to hurting me, the less we'll have to fight off everyone who wants to return her to that tower."

"Sorry, my liege, I didn't mean that. I just meant that she's Seelie. This will not go over well."

Well, fuck all of—

"No," Kane says flatly. "She's not."

I jerk my head up. "*What?*"

Oh… shit. This explains everything. He has the wrong person. He has to think I'm someone else.

Before I can flinch away, Kane reaches out and brushes my hair aside, fingertips grazing the back of my lower neck, pushing my head to reveal the skin there. "This," he says, voice grave, "is not a birthmark. It's a shroud."

My gaze moves all over the floor as if the understanding of what he said is written there, and every second counts. It's true I have a birthmark there, but not being a Seelie? He *has* to have the wrong person.

Or…

"How did you know it was there?"

"Your lady's maid confirmed it for me."

He can't do this. Break my identity like this. He could be lying with so much ease, and I have no means of proving him wrong. This is the largest fuckery of my mind I've experienced in—

"If she's Unseelie," Freya begins, like a true general in someone's militia who accepts what they've been

91

told. "They'll all want to claw at her to make her their mate. To take that from Silas—"

"I'm aware," Kane says darkly. I can hear the lethal promise buried beneath the calm. "I will take care of it if it becomes too much."

I look up at him, almost nervous. I've *never* looked to someone like their sheer presence will save me, except for my adoptive mother. I don't even know Kane. But if, somehow, I'm not a Seelie, then this woman is right, and I'm not just fresh meat to the people here, I'm a delicate slice of marbled flesh. Kane catches my gaze for a breathless second. Something almost like regret flashes through his face, then shutters away.

Without waiting, he leaves—a storm of a man wrapped in chains he's ready to break. Freya jerks her chin at me, but I can hardly process my surroundings as my heart pounds in my ears. I feel so cold, alone, and also more alive than I ever did under Silas's rule.

All the while, I touch the back of my neck, staring blankly at the floor.

"Why did Silas send you here?" Freya asks, her tone cutting, but the way she looks me over, I can tell she's far more curious.

Stumbling slightly to the nearest chair, my stomach feels as taut as ship rope. "I, uh... I was instructed to heal Kane," I say quietly, my eyes still gyrating in my skull like I've unlearned the ability to focus. "Silas said I either come back broken, or I don't return." My voice is as cold as these walls, realizing if I mate with Kane, it would *enrage* the Seelie High Lord.

Even in this dead, crumbling place, where the walls bleed sorrowful tales, I finally feel the hollow ache of possibility clawing at my ribs. Some part of my mind registers in many ways there *has* to be many hidden truths to my identity. Or maybe it's just the trauma of being confined that finds comfort in *belonging* to someone...

Does it matter? Mating Kane could be my ultimate revenge against Silas.

I'll deal with my identity crisis later, a trauma I can't begin to unfold right now.

Hope—that bittersweet bitch—is back.

Freya frowns, sitting down near me after locking the door with many bolts and a wooden barrier. "Why?"

"I'm not marriage material for High Lords. I've ruined five proposals and four arrangements." My voice is a little stronger now.

"There will be jealousy, for your information," she mutters through a quiet sigh. "Kane is highly sought after among the Unseelie."

"Great, just what I need."

She snickers. "I'm just warning you. It's not my role to question him *too* much, but others will when he's not around. Ignore it for now until we're in a better setting where it can be properly addressed."

It seems the world's the same, no matter what side of the wall one finds themselves on. Everyone always hated me as soon as I was paired with *desirable* suitors, and then they were sickly sweet when those proposals fell through.

Sitting here is one of the most boring encounters as silence stretches while Freya moves to sit next to the door. No one comes near, that much I can smell. I can only stare at the same table for so long before the tension of everything presses against my chest with a reminder so firm it could be carved into stone—even if I'm free of Silas, I do *not* belong here.

Do I even belong *anywhere*?

I can't stop touching the back of my neck… it's seriously not a birthmark?

I'm busy biting the inside of my cheek when a scent hits me before Kane even enters. Dark spice. Bloodied steel. Something ancient and wild enough to sink teeth into my nerves.

For a moment, before I see him enter the room, I think I may have dreamed everything. That perhaps I read the room wrong and fell victim to Kane's manipulation, that even his scent could be some trick, some slow, cruel way to unravel me.

When he enters the room, I don't look at him. The more I think about it, the more positive I am that he *is* messing with me. Instead, I notice how Freya behaves with him like Lawrence did with Silas. It's the only thing about Kane that feels familiar to me. That cold dominance. That unstated threat.

"Mockingbird is successful," he states.

I'm on my feet faster than I'd like to have been. The habit of moving swiftly when a High Lord speaks is a hard one to break. Kane moves slowly toward me, grabbing my arm as he turns to Freya. "Follow closely."

The touch of his hand sears through the fabric of my sleeve. Having such little space between us is distracting, nearly pressing against such a muscled mass of capability. Once we're among more of his people, their vicious gazes hotly raking over me, I confirm to myself that no matter what, I'm far from achieving any ounce of safety. "What's happening?" I grind out, trying to claim some control here.

A few Unseelie look at me like I've just done something terrible for speaking to him in such a way. When their gazes flit up to Kane, they immediately face back ahead and focus on something else.

Kane doesn't reply as, the stone ceilings soaring up into a network of ancient archways. "Why did they look at me like that?" I ask once there's enough distance between us. "I mean, other than the obvious. I feel like I'm missing a social cue and would rather not stand out more than I already do."

"You asked me a question," he says without pausing.

"Are people not allowed to ask you questions?"

"No. They ask Freya or Osman."

"Why?" I ask, pursing my lips out of decorum now that I know this isn't allowed. Old habits truly die hard. Not even Silas was this strict.

"It's not how I desire to reign. Not right now, anyway. My presence should command without a single word. It works best among people who are starving for change."

There's something about that statement that hits me all at once. He's a real being, with desires, motives, and strategy. And an ego. My mind immediately aligns him with all the others I met, all the Lords and those that the world reveres from the outside. So many fail to realize they're just mortals, even if they live longer than humans. They obey their own desires like the rest of us.

I fell to that very enigma from Kane, like I'm a commoner.

Panic bubbles like a rolling pot of water that is about to burst in a blooping mess. The only thing to calm me down is knowing that I have to get over it. Silas was sending me to Faust next, so how is this worse?

Survival.

I *must* reorient my mind if I am to reign triumphant. Mating Kane is a victory compared to the alternative. Fated reasoning, or not.

My shoulders square as I allow him to guide me, holding my head tall. We enter into a vast rotunda, the ceiling stretching high above us into a dome of stained stone and black iron. Thousands of prisoners line the walls, stories upon stories, cages and cells stacked like a grotesque hive.

Kane stops in the center of it all. The ground seems

to *thrum* under my boots. Many of his people fan out, unlocking the cells in something that appears rehearsed. The metallic shriek of opening doors fills the air, thickening it, electrifying it. "A change is coming!" Kane bellows, voice booming through the chamber, commanding absolute, trembling silence.

Freed prisoners drift forward to the railings, clinging to the bars, clinging to hope.

"The Seelie will fall, and *I* will be standing among their ashes, wearing a *new* crown." He turns slowly, allowing those words to soak into the marrow of every soul in the room. "If your cell has been opened, you are free to follow my people. If you choose not to follow us and go your own path—know this: the duskborn are mine now. They will hunt down any betrayer. Give me no reason to hate you, and you'll never see me again." He lifts his chin slightly, a sovereign accepting inevitable loyalty. "The rest of you," he says, voice dipping into pure ice, "will rot in your cages until your final breath."

A beat of stunned silence—and then chaos. Screams. Metal slamming against stone. The air explodes into violent noises. Kane grabs my arm again, unbothered by the bedlam, and hauls me back through the crumbling hallways.

My mind spins the entire time, overanalyzing everything.

Get off this island. Get away from Silas. That's all that matters.

I could plan an escape later, once we're far enough away. The thought barely has time to root itself before I feel a sharp, burning prick at my neck. I turn, startled— the last thing I see are the metallic eyes of Kane as everything goes black.

Kane

Chapter 9

Holding Victoria against me is dangerous. The bond strains between us like a taut wire, vibrating, begging to place my attention solely on her—on what should have been sealed long ago.

It takes everything I have to rip my attention away and move. Carrying her close, I stride with purpose through these tunnels. The decision to incapacitate her was made swiftly. The debauchery for flesh and violence that will follow until we get to land is not something she needs to witness. Already, the halls and tunnels fill with those who take advantage of their gifted freedom. The way a person screams when violated, either through flesh or murder, is not a sound one forgets.

Victoria is only here because of Silas, and I will *not* let this place be her introduction into the new world. The duskborn will handle the aftermath of this place and what it does to people.

Victoria's body is slack against mine, her head nestled beneath my chin, her lashes kissing the tops of her cheeks as if in surrender. Let them look. Let every eye on the battlements and every whisper in the shadows spread the message that Victoria is mine now. And I do not forgive for any harm brought to her. Let the tale race ahead to Silas's ears—that the woman he caged like a relic now lies safely against the chest of the man who will destroy him. Of the man he tried to throw to the Carrows.

I hope he trembles. I hope he clutches the iron arms of his throne and finally understands fear. He will either step into the open, or I will storm that fucking castle.

He will pay for sending her *here*.

As we breach the gates of Carrows, the sky itself seems to shift. The light of day hits my skin like absolution, like fire after endless dark. The movements are swift around me as the plan of action commences. The longboats wait at the levee, bobbing in solemn rhythm. I get Victoria onto the largest longboat, unmarked, ignoring the oarsmen as they stare at her while I move to the back of the vessel near the mast at the stern. I lay her against other fabrics, adjusting the ones around her so she won't move too greatly, her olive skin a beautiful contrast against the surroundings, including her inky black hair.

Even unconscious, she unsettles me. So delicate...

yet every part of her has the strength of a kingdom denied its crown. She will sit by my side as we undo the injustice of this world.

I settle beside her, hand still pressed lightly to her ribcage, feeling the rise and fall of her breath. It's already rising and falling faster than it should, meaning she's been exposed to this before.

The unbound energy of desperate revenge tests my resolve. What did they do to her while unconscious? How often did it happen that she has some build-up to its effects?

Osman joins our vessel while Freya remains behind to direct the rest. My gaze rakes across the oarsmen until they look away, understanding without needing to be told—she is not to be touched. Not even by thought. Not until she can command that herself and is fully bonded to me. "No more delays. Freya will handle the rest. Get this ship out of here."

There was once a plan. Wait. Regroup. Ensure the others made it. But that plan shattered the moment Victoria fell limp in my arms. Now, nothing else matters.

We're leaving immediately.

I cast one final glance up at the looming silhouette of Carrows, to the place Silas thought he entombed me. My jaw tightens when considering it's a place he meant to entomb Victoria.

How poetic it will be when he learns who walked out, and *who* he has in his arms.

My only regret is that I will not see the moment his mask cracks—when he realizes what he's lost. When he sees *her* free… and wrapped in the arms of the man who will drag his reign into the dust.

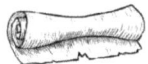

THE BOAT ROCKS against the pier with a hollow thud, the black water slapping against the wood. Mist clings to the surface, rising to mix with the thick, sour air of fish, rust, and salt.

A second dose was needed when Victoria started to rouse. In the event of an emergency, there's a counter tonic that can be wiped under her nose to aggressively pull her from her sleep. I can't have her awake and worried. It demands too much from me, the unsealed bond festering. I need to get us safely on land before worrying about her place here.

Beyond the docks, the port is alive. Filled with any and all who will smell her. There's an undertone of whatever true identity she is, but it's utterly stained with the life she has lived. From the foods she's eaten to the oils used in her hair.

Give it a few weeks before the stain of the Seelie's will be removed from her. And those beautiful, golden hazel eyes will burn *bright* with vengeance.

Vendors shout from behind their stalls, hawking

goods as shady as the buyers themselves. The buildings are stacked crooked and close, wood bleached gray by endless storms. Ships groan in the harbor, their rigging snapping when tugged.

My people leap lightly onto the dock as I lift Victoria into my arms—she will be waking any moment—and carry her with a care that makes my own men glance at each other. Let them. The sooner they connect these dots, the better.

A man waits near the makeshift, short gangway, flanked by guards with polished armor and blank stares.

He doesn't fit here. His clothes are too fine—dark green velvet slashed with gold thread, a long coat meant for a throne room, not the piss-stinking docks.

An outfit *I* wear when necessary.

A half-smile plays on his lips like he already thinks he's won whatever game he's here to play. Ignoring him, I take Victoria to Freya, where a horse-drawn carriage lined with hay awaits. As I lay her down, my arms still underneath her and her face closer to mine, Victoria's slow beating heart is no longer felt against my skin.

She is warm, alive, real.

She's just a stranger to me, in truth, but the *promise* of what she is to me is as mesmerizing as it is to dethrone the Seelie. "Whistle if she awakens," I say to Freya, leaving her but not too far.

Lord Malric's smile tightens as I approach him, his gaze flitting over to the carriage. Something deep and aggressive within me wants to lock that woman away until every last rite of mating and bonding has been fulfilled. *Control yourself.*

"So, the rumors of you escaping are true. Kane Blackthorn himself, completely dismantling the Carrows. It's like dragging a legend out of the sea." He gestures lazily to the guards, pretending not to stare. "And through my little mice, I've heard you have the adopted daughter with you. And that happens to look *exactly* like her description."

My voice is flat. "Rumors spread faster than changing winds."

He laughs once—a high, brittle sound like glass cracking. He steps nearer, but doesn't get too close, as I still hold the rank here. "Whoever marries her is entitled to Silas's protection," he says quietly. "She's been diffi-cult to marry, I've heard. But now, some of those who rejected her are talking about returning out of despera-tion, knowing what looms in the air."

I study him without blinking. This is the kind of man who thinks words are weapons because of the networking of whispering spies he has. A wild card, I acknowledge, but he holds no *power.*

"Do you go around often making vague statements without defining what you mean?" I ask, my tone soft enough to be dangerous. "Because you are wasting my time, and I've spent too many fucking nights in that prison to waste it *gossiping* with you."

The man's throat bobs as he swallows.

"I don't know why you have her," he mutters, lowering his voice even further, "but either get rid of her, or figure out a way to make her permanently unavailable. I don't want that kind of trouble near me."

I let the silence stretch just long enough to make him sweat. Then I smile—sharp and cold. "I already planned on it."

He bows his head slightly and takes a careful step back. Turning away from the Lord and his guards, I stride back to the carriage as my boots leave prints in the wet soil. Behind me, the port churns and roars, oblivious to the small war just narrowly avoided.

But it doesn't matter.

Bigger battles wait ahead.

And I have every intention of winning.

Victoria

Chapter 10

My mind is blank.

When my eyes open, I'm completely unaware as to where I am. This isn't the typical room I wake up in, nor does it smell like me— *him*. Is it a letter? Did I sleep with it under my pillow?

The recollection of the Carrows returns, but it's such a bizarre suggestion I'm still convinced I dreamed it. There had been Kane...

Sitting up in a bed that is most definitely not my own, I eye the worn quilt with furrowed brows. Licking dry lips, I search for water—I nearly jump out of my skin, my heart profusely beating, when I see *he's* sitting near me, in a chair, with no shirt on. We stare at each other for a while, the dim lighting creating a confusing intimacy, at least for me, as I don't often have people in my bedroom at this hour. "What happened?" I croak, my voice dry.

He nods to the table next to me, where a massive water bladder teases me as I greedily uncork and down it. There's nothing ladylike in my approach, and when I'm done, I don't bother apologizing for such crass behavior.

If my memory is reliable at all, he knocked me out.

In all my years of observing the masks that people wear, and how those can slip in the slightest ways when someone finally feels alone, I can tell Kane has a mask that has slipped. To the average observer, his expression is still stolid. But not his eyes, that's always the first to slip.

It reminds me exactly of the times when my adoptive siblings would shut the door, and then their eyes would come to life with the *true* person inside.

"Care to answer me?" I ask, completely tossing my *own* mask. "What happened?"

"You were given a sedative," he smoothly replies.

My first reaction disappoints me. I'm not even mad, or surprised. Silas has used things like this on me many times, and I'm used to it as a form of communication. But how deranged is that? That this is okay to me? "Silas did that to me many times, you know."

His eyes flare, and dare I say something personal crosses his face with the way he juts his jaw forward slightly. "Were you hurt during those times?" he slowly asks.

"Not that I know of." It's so quiet in here that my

voice almost sounds funny. "I'm just saying this feels exactly like *home*."

His eyes flare even more, adjusting slightly in his chair, reminding me of how broad his body is. "It will *never* be like that."

"Yes, because sedating me is such a romantic gesture," I quip, looking out the window next to me to see where I am. I'm trying my damndest to completely ignore the intoxicating scent of Kane, or the way his voice is like pouring honeyed wine into my ears.

"That was the *least* of my concerns. The scenes that followed were shocking and I didn't want you to see that. Carrying you off had the added benefit that kept others away."

"And why's that?" I ask, only seeing a dirt pathway and some trees outside this window.

"I don't think I've *ever* carried someone like that in front of my people."

I toss the quilt off, the coarse wool falling into a heap beside me as if shedding a second skin. That guzzle of water seems to have given me new life. "I'm *not* to be used like how that castle used me," I snap, swinging my legs over the edge as my feet meet the cold, wooden floor. "I'm not to be used at *all*." I glare up at him. If he expected me pliant, he's about ten years too late. "I want to leave. Right now. I already know exactly where I want to go to get as far away from these court politics as possible."

He studies me with something that borders on

amusement. "No." He inhales through his nose, his shoulders rising with the action as he shrugs. "Or fine, go ahead. You'll find that I follow you."

Perhaps years with Silas *have* been good for me, teaching me how to live under pressure. How to *breathe* within it. So I don't get angry. I don't even scowl. I just *think*. "Where are we?" I ask, needing the lay of the land.

My impassive attitude does not speak for my motives. I simply am aware that being a hot head is not the best way to lead in a conversation, nor to assess. I search around this space with my gaze, examining the typical stonework, a hearth with old ash, fading rugs, heavy beams, and a table coated with dust.

"An Unseelie Lord has granted us into his piers, and we are currently in an unoccupied dwelling."

"Why is it unoccupied?"

"The family relocated."

My gaze flits back to him, my body stiffening when I'm firmly reminded he is definitely still in this room. "Where to?"

His lips spread into a crooked grin—his presence is just as distracting as his letters. "They relocated to *my* lands, seeing as how he owes fealty to me. There are quite a lot of people coming to me right now, even while I was in the Carrows."

And just like that, the metaphorical wings of mine that Silas believes he clipped are spread wide by Kane. One thing is probably certain—I don't think I'm going back to that castle. "Why are you in here with me?" I ask, looking him over. No weapons. He has a belt but no holsters.

"You know why."

That sends the most unpleasantly wonderful chills down my spine, the burning desire from when we exchanged letters nearly scalding hot. "At some point, you have to leave," I say, trying to figure out how I get a chance alone. Silas could keep an eye on me because I was in his *castle*. But here? There's a chance to flee. A chance to disappear among the trees.

I'm so close to the woods, it's almost mocking me.

Kane's fingers wrap around the armrest of his chair, gripping it as he rises. I have been alone for far too long, because the image of his veined hands and arms flexing should never, under any circumstances, be *this* tantalizing. It's as if the things I feel never even bother passing through my brain. They merely *exist*.

The bastard even takes a step near me, and I scoot back onto the bed, propped on my knees so I can spring away if necessary. Silvery eyes bore into mine as he tucks his chin down to look at me. "It has not gone unnoticed that you are currently completely unclaimed and outside Silas's purview. It is *already* an issue."

The animal within purrs at the idea of him staking a claim, which furthers my belief that something is wrong with me. That scent—that damn smell—makes it worse. "I do not have to be claimed," I say, shocked at how wrong that statement feels.

He tilts his head. "Unfortunately for your sense of freedom, you do. You are *the* way into Silas's perceived protection. Unless you have an army hiding in the woods to defend you, you need to use someone else's."

I know exactly what he means, as I've considered it so many times. I'm painfully aware that without another castle to hide within, Silas *will* come for me. "I didn't ask for *any* of this," I grind out, slightly baring my teeth. "How am I supposed to know what's the best decision to make?"

He quirks a brow. "You're in luck that your mate happens to have an army."

Oh, I don't like what those words do for me. I rise to my feet on the bed, just barely avoiding touching the ceiling with my head, looking *down* at him now. "You're so *certain* of this declaration."

"Oh *yes*, because we are," he replies, almost as if he finds this humorous. "And *yes*, we will make that bond solid. You will then hide behind *my* army."

"Either you're an idiot or naive, because a mating bond requires *consent*," I quip, wanting to scratch his face. Then bathe my skin in his musk and bite his neck —*no!* My gaze flits up to the door...

"I can be persuasive," he says with even a hint of play.

Glaring back into those eyes that confuse the shit out of me, I ask, "Why are you doing this to me?"

"*I* can't even protect you among my people, little flower," he calmly replies, perhaps even gently. "Not

114

unless you are *bound* to me, and I bound to you. But that clearly cannot happen in such a short time, and you also cannot leave this house until there's no doubt what you are going to mean to me. You're very familiar with court politics, which means you understand why this is a pressing matter."

Mean to him. It suggests a sense of caring. Like a spindle turning ferociously, my mind spins the possibility of a life where he *is* my mate and is bound through fate to actually take care of me. Love me. Defend me. Honor me.

And as I stare down at the man that somewhere inside of me knows he's my mate, I'm met with paralysis. He seems to have cleaned off some of the grime from the Carrows, but the wound is still fresh on his stomach. He hasn't even been free for an entire day and is already planning on bonding with me. "How can we be mates—" I breathe out, struggling to get the remainder out. Saying it aloud shatters the foundation I've built my identity on.

If he's Unseelie, and we are mates… my hand mindlessly rises to the back of my neck, the birthmark existing as long as I can remember. The answer is so obvious and brings so much understanding to my life that I cannot deny it further.

Am I… Unseelie?

Kane doesn't move toward me, or reach out. He just stares with what feels like an invasion into my soul. "When we had our very brief encounter, I've never been so affected by another's scent. Nor has someone maintained my rapt attention like you have. It didn't take long to piece it together, but I didn't understand how a Seelie could be fated to an Unseelie. With whatever turn of the fates, the Carrows held the answers, and I researched all I could and learned of the binding tattoos.

"I then made a request to your lady's maid in a letter penned just for her, and she confirmed the tattoo on your neck and what it looked like—" my eyes widen, remembering when she touched it while braiding my hair and asked how long I've had it "—and while I don't know the circumstances for your arrival at Silas's court, I can easily surmise you were not taken from a Seelie home."

The concept is painfully liberating. I *knew* I didn't belong, and yet this means my identity is rooted with creatures I've been told to hate. "Who *am* I then?" I ask, my voice trembling more than I care for.

"Your body and soul have been criminally neglected, Victoria," he says, raising one of his hands out as if I should take it and get off the bed, the request suggesting so many simultaneous things. "*I* will be your liberator."

I didn't know Kane was so socially fluent. Whatever part of me craved him while alone in my tower is absolutely gluttonous with everything he just said. I swallow thickly. "You have a war at your doorsteps to navigate, Kane. Why not just lock me away until it's done?"

He holds the hand closer, the tips of my fingers rising as if I want to throw all caution to the wind.

"I crave this connection more than I want to admit. My attention to detail will be severely impacted until you are taken care of first."

Through unexplained understandings, I *know* Kane can feel me giving in. I can sense it through the way the tips of his fingers reach out further to graze mine, as if proving that his touch can be gentle. My hand slides into his while I stare him in the eyes, trying desperately to discern what's true.

His skin against mine is foreign, yet familiar. Like a warmth I didn't know I was missing. "I know much better than this," I say, although I truthfully don't care at all.

The left corner of his mouth tilts up slightly into the smallest smile. "And yet you wrote me that letter."

"I don't know a thing about you," I quip, like a drowning man sucking in water before he succumbs.

"We will have plenty of time to learn."

I grip his hand tighter, and something needy flashes in his eyes. For whatever reason, holding this much power over him fills me with a new kind of purpose. "Please just answer this truthfully—what exactly do you want from me? I am familiar with arranged partnership. I don't mind knowing what you *truly* want from this. I'll —" *damn it all.* "I'll agree to this as long as you're honest with me. Please just give me that."

I swear there's a low grumble that emanates from his chest, gripping my hand in return as he raises it up to his face, slowly running my skin along his nose to breathe me in. I'm utterly weak at the knees for such a simple gesture. "I've had two years to contemplate what a fated connection would mean. I admit, I grew greedy over time." Silver eyes flash up at mine. "I want the deep bond that is promised, for your body and heart to be my reprieve. To utterly trust and love someone, and have it be returned. For that, I'll hand you the entirety of any kingdom you desire."

What do I say to that? The man has ensnared me since I first saw him, imprisoned by all the things my imagination could conjure. Now he's *here*, holding my hand, telling me things I've only ever heard in dreams.

"Just don't hurt me," I say, even quieter.

"If we solidify the bond, you will have every leverage to break me, little flower. Hurting you would be the end of me."

That's the kind of bargain I can feel safe within. The more I observe him, the more it's clear that he *also* seems to be under a spell. Unlike me, he seems to embrace it. And *I* want it. I want it so badly I'm terrified of it not existing, which means I'm pushing it away so the disappointment is only minimal.

But... I'm done questioning my life.

I nod at him, and lean slightly forward to show I want down. Placing my other hand in his, he helps me onto the floor. "Did whatever you sedate me with have anything else laced in it?" I ask, feeling the heat in my cheeks. "Anything to aid in persuasion?"

His grin continues to melt me. "No, that's the faintest existence of our bond, desperate to unite."

My brows raise. "It's desperate alright."

He raises that hand of mine back to his face and brushes his lips against my skin. The heat of his breath and mouth against my flesh may as well be the final act of seduction. My entire arm nearly goes limp at such a gesture, having *never* been so swept off my feet by *any* suitor. He then raises those liquid silver eyes to meet mine, smirking at what must be the effect he has on me. When he releases my hand, I almost want to slap him for not following through. Sure, I had hoped, when younger, that whoever Silas chose for me would somehow magically be a perfectly romantic partner.

To actually feel *desire* for someone that I choose.

And now I want *this* man.

Kane moves to the bedside table, opening a black leather bag to remove a vial—flecked with pearlescence —holding it between his fingers as he turns around to present it to me.

"What is this?"

"The moon's serum."

My gaze snaps to his. We both share a silent conversation, because this is more than just biting my neck. This initiates *the* bond, allowing his bite to be one of many steps to bring us to permanence in an ancient rite.

What shocks me the most is that I want to rip it from his hands and down it all. *Let* him bite me. This is the most romance I've gotten in my entire life, and he's right, to feign Silas, I need an army. And mating with Kane would be the *perfect* revenge. And if the fates care about me at all, I'll get to enjoy my days rather than loathe them.

It's not as if the concept of marrying a man for my freedom is new to me. If anything, this is an opportunity I don't want to waste.

Taking it from his hand, I uncork it with a soft pop. With my other hand, I pinch the side of my finger so I can dig my fang into it, a bubble of blood forming that drips into the vial.

The scent from inside is wild—feral and sweet, like moonlight on bloodied stone.

"Well," he murmurs, eyes narrowing with pleased surprise. "You're quite eager."

"Kiss my hand like that more often and I'll grow into this without a problem," I say, handing it to him with my head held high. "I don't want to go back to Silas. And you're right, if I go out there without belonging to any court, then it's only a matter of time."

He chuckles low in his throat, piercing his own finger with the same precision—no wince, no pause. His blood meets mine inside the vial like two rivers converging. "And what was your initial plan?"

"I was going to somehow make it to the Everwoods."

"That's two months of riding on horseback."

"I know," I sigh, shame brushing the edges of my voice. "I've never even been outside the castle alone. Honestly, I'd have been caught in the first week. But... I was willing to give it my all."

He doesn't gloat. He simply drinks—half the vial, head tilting slightly as the serum slides down his throat. Then he offers the rest to me.

I hold the half-emptied thing, hesitating when considering all those who follow him will have to sacrifice something for me. "And you're okay with having your court defend me?"

"I'm in need of a suitor, and taking you would provoke Silas enough that I think half my people would support it just for that alone."

I tip the vial back and drink. Fire and starlight twist down my throat, blooming inside my chest like I've just watered a plant that's been waiting for its nectar. "So, we're both doing this to piss off Silas?"

A sharp, haunted anger flashes in his eyes. "It's a common denominator for acting swiftly, but we're both here because of the pulse between us. Don't ever forget that."

My breath comes deeper now, slower. I'm transported back to that first, ink-smudged letter I dared to send him, how my hand trembled, how my heart didn't. It's like being stained in his scent finally lets my mind be a little freer, not as obsessed with closing the distance.

"It won't be a problem remembering when you haunted me nearly every night."

That deeper hunger, almost vulnerable, appears in his eyes again. My lips slightly part, that surge of *need* returning, and it's then that he wraps that hand around the nape of my neck as if it's always belonged on my body. There's no time to think about it before his fangs pierce my flesh, my body tensing. The heat of his mouth and my blood make me gasp, which turns to a whimper when he digs deeper for the sake of it before he pulls back, licking my neck so pain and pleasure uncomfortably intertwine.

When he finally pulls back, I see it written in his eyes that something has changed between us, irrevocably.

"There's no second vial," I realize out loud.

He licks my blood from his lips. "You'll return it once you're within my court."

The strangest thing happens within me. It's as if I can feel what my presence does to him, and a deep, concerning need within me wants to kiss him terribly. "You really do want me," I say, the reassurance in such a sensation, the final act of approval I needed.

"Is that surprising?"

"I've never been wanted for *me*," I confess, like cleaning out an old wound. What would that be like? To have a man want my affection because it's *mine*?

I don't realize I'm almost lightheaded until he raises a hand to gently grip my jaw, thumb brushing just over my bottom lip, the first physical interaction to suggest something *more*. His eyes search mine, not for permission because he knows he already has that, but for connection. And gods help me, I give it freely.

Because something inside me is cracking open.

I've been locked in rooms and choked by silence. But here, Kane is the male who wrote me letters soaked in longing. He sees me. He sees *only* me.

The space between us lessens, but he doesn't rush this, like I'll vanish if he moves too fast.

I meet him halfway.

His lips tentatively brush mine, and when I don't pull away—when I clutch his arm like a lifeline—he kisses me like it's a slow, reverent claiming.

And for the first time in my life, I don't feel stolen.

I feel chosen.

I swear I can sense the starving part of him latching onto the promise of affection that this bond will give, and perhaps we've both been starved of the same nourishment despite living very different lives. My lips move with his guidance, his deep groans melting my bones. I may be inexperienced, but I'm not ignorant. I've explored my own body, and I know what his mouth and cock can do.

Stiffening slightly when I realize just how far my mind is willing to wander, it's as if the bond assuages me with the reminder that his scent—all over—will spread fast through rumors.

Oh, the idea of the entirety of the Seelie court realizing who I've chosen, after rejecting all of them, is as tantalizing as Kane's scent. My true identity doesn't even seem relevant, not if this is the life I choose. I press harder into the kiss, his groan greeting me with approval. Those rough hands roam lower around the small of my back, and the sensation of being within the arms of someone so appealing and dangerous is absolutely feral within my system.

I'm a flower that's stolen warmth from fading rays of sunshine, and now I'm finally standing out in the middle of a cloudless day to absorb the sun. I smile into the kiss, enamored to know it's *Kane* who will deflower me.

My clothes are removed as enigmatically as his—they were once on our bodies, and now they're piled onto the floor—through an intense exchange of heat, teeth slightly clashing, and his tongue claiming my mouth like a prelude to what he'll do with my body. An intense high shrouds every bit of common sense. While utterly cocooned in his strength as he holds me close, his cock grazes my belly, and my lower jaw trembles with need. Even if some part of this feels utterly empty due to the lack of knowing him, at least Silas won't be able to sell me as a prized *virgin* anymore.

Kane is quick to change our positions as my balance is off kilter when I tumble back onto the bed, the man standing next to it with a firm and commanding erection. Oh, I never knew just the *sight* of this could make me come completely undone, knowing its intention is for *me*.

"You do understand," he begins, glowering. "That we are bound in ways so archaic that few recall it?" He moves from the side of the bed to the bottom, leaning over to reach forward with those veined, calloused hands to grip my hips, sliding me down so my legs part on either side of him. I gasp at how easy that was for him, waiting for my flesh to collide with his, but it never happens. No, instead, he kneels down, his shoulders the same height as my knees. Rough hands spread my legs further, and it's the vulnerability in this exposure that breaks through the fog of fucking. "And you will only fuck me as your mate, little flower, *not* to enrage Silas."

Perhaps I *can* feel how much he wants this for himself, because he can apparently read my heart as if the words are scrawled between my breasts. I don't know what to say, and when my legs begin to instinctively close, he parts them open with a force I could never counter. With a force that confusingly sparks more of my arousal. "Do you agree?"

This… this is really happening…

"Yes," I breathe out with a sinful desire.

"For our binding, not to spite anyone else?" he asks, sliding that massive hand over my inner thigh in almost a caress. "I want to *feel* you mean it. I know you can feel what I want, and I can certainly feel you."

Feel. Yes… I can actually feel what matters to him.

It's a consideration that exists without effort inside my mind, compartmentalized into Kane.

Your mate, Victoria. For the male whose teeth marks will permanently scar your skin.

"For *you*," I say, drunk on infatuation.

The idea of pleasing my mate, even if *he* is unmarked, is like smoothing out a string that connects us, playing it without friction. He dips his head down, breathing me in. Without hesitation, his tongue deeply presses against me, my moan completely involuntary as a sensation I've never felt streaks through me. The way his hand grips and dips into my thighs brings a pleasure I've never known. Every sound I make pushes him to work harder, my fingers spreading out as I want to touch him while the wet heat of his mouth mixes with every sensitive edge... but grabbing him with greed feels foreign, improper.

"Touch me, Victoria," he growls.

Within seconds, I grip the top of his hand, my lips trembling as a familiar burst of ecstasy rises, brought on completely without any effort on my end.

Your mate is pleasing you.

I whimper.

I whimper *again*.

This is happening much faster than when I'm by myself. "Kane," I moan, still getting used to the sound coming from my mouth.

"Louder," he commands through a suck, almost as if it the command wasn't voluntary.

"Fuck," I mutter. "*Kane!*"

My navel tightens as my knees close around him, Kane grunting as he drains my orgasm, his hands nearly bruising my hips with how hard he grips me.

And I can feel him. The desire to fuck me without pausing or grace. To dominate my body in ways that will permanently imprint him on me. I don't know what's happening to me, but I say, "I want you to fuck me how you want to."

He growls as he stands, murderous hands gripping my hips once more. If I were to rise, I bet my scent would be all over that magnificently masculine face. I don't get to find out as my legs are spread around his waist. The tip of his cock aligns with my body as I'm still caught in the wakes of pleasure.

"You're so beautiful," he says, his pupils completely blown. Without a second to waste, I gasp as he completely spreads me open with a gentle thrust forward. I watch as his cock slowly disappears into my body, feeling that invasion from the inside.

His girth has me taking a few deep breaths to help my body accept him, my eyes rolling with how it feels to be utterly filled with Kane, like no crevice is left untouched.

I'm only more excited by the idea that this actually is happening—Kane has taken *this* part of me. I'm never returning to that castle again... only to wherever this brute of a man takes me.

I've heard losing one's womanhood can hurt, but I

didn't quite know what that would mean. My whimper mixes with groans of pleasure more than pain.

He leans down to kiss me as he gently slides in and out of me, holding me very still, until all at once his tongue possessively swoops into my mouth as his cock *buries* into me, completely filling me with him as he groans into my mouth.

Kane's hips move harder, the bed rhythmically hitting the wall of a stranger's home as he moans while our flesh collides. I'm amazed at how I feel another orgasm rising, sounds of pleasure mixing with his.

"Come on my cock, Victoria, as I spill into you."

Some part of me wonders if I'm so unrestrained because he's my mate, or simply because of the novelty. Either way, I dig my fingers into his thick, hard back, kissing him as I *want* to come again. To use this violent man for my pleasure.

When my body is on the verge of coming once more, Kane presses his warm lips down my jaw, licking the fresh wounds of his claiming mark. My orgasm mixes with searing pain as I cry out, so overwhelmed with pleasure at the notion that it will be impossible to hide this mating mark.

He thrusts with so much force that he's utterly flush against me. I'm so full of Kane when until his cock pulsates. It dawns on me that he's actually coming inside of me, and I'll be leaking the scent of a revered Unseelie High Lord.

I doubt I'll exist much without this claim for some

time. The tether between us tightens and thickens, this bite permanently intertwining our energies so only death can separate us. The behemoth gently kisses me after unleashing what has to be only a glimpse at the feral side of him, my blood on his lips.

"You are mine, little flower. The rest of the world may fear me, but not you. You will *never* need to."

Victoria

Epilogue

Whether or not hope remains to be an elusive, fickle creature is yet to be determined. Personally, I think sheer will is ignored more than it otherwise should be. *Hope* may have gotten me through the darkest nights, held up by a desperate need to prevent surrendering myself to the courts of someone who loathed me.

The courts that I never *belonged* to.

Now, standing tall in what was once the sanctum of this Seelie palace, it gives me great pleasure to wear a violet dress adorned with metal. The fabric flows effortlessly to the hem that stops at my ankles. A lady's suit of armor. I spent weeks wondering what to wear upon returning here, as a dress, after all, is what *they* taught me to wear. Made me perform in.

But Kane, in all the glory of his brilliant heart, persuaded me that I'm allowed to love things I found within these walls without letting them define me. To *not* wear an outfit such as this would not be honoring the authentic side of me. So, I'm honoring myself in my own way with metal plating sewn into the shoulders, corset, and sides.

The corridor leading to Silas's private quarters is just as I remember, with immaculately polished floors, gold-veined columns, and light spilling like the opulent windows.

How many secrets these walls have silenced.

My heels click with deliberate poise on the marble as I approach the double doors. I had chosen this location, as well. It's where he first hit me, where he told me I was a healer but my locket would be locked away, and where he had been given the notice that Kane was freed.

Ginger was kind enough to relay that to me, and is now happily my lady's maid underneath Kane.

Perhaps this place *did* offer me a few things worth keeping.

As I stand in front of these doors, a lifetime of sorrow, regret, anger, damaged hope, and a longing for just being *wanted*—my eyes fall to the gilded knobs.

The footsteps that had trailed my shadow stop just behind me.

Kane doesn't ask why I've stopped. Not now, not all these months later, with our bond completed. The bond between us hums like a tether of heat and strength at my back. He knows I hesitate because an oddly childish part of me is worried I'll say the wrong thing. Ruin the moment I'm so eager to claim.

Moment.

No, I'm done having those with Silas.

Opening the doors, I step forward into a room with half the curtains drawn, dust hanging in the sun's rays. For once, the pristine High Lord of the Seelie looks small. His face is bloodied, his clothes ripped apart and barely clinging to his skin. When his blue eyes lift to meet mine, for once, I believe this really will be the last time I have to look at them. "Hello, Silas."

He barks a laugh and spits on the antique rug beneath him. "You fucking whore of a betrayer."

Behind me, I hear Kane's slow, measured footsteps as he enters. The sound alone shifts Silas's attention. I watch the flicker of fear cross his features, masked instantly by an arrogance that he will more than likely die with.

"Now now, that's just your bruised ego speaking," I murmur. "Don't worry about Kane. It's *my* choice on what happens to you."

A dozen emotions flash in his eyes—fear, confusion, manipulation. "Victoria. After everything... I *did* house you. I *did* give you the clothing, my own children—"

"You stole me from my family," I say, my voice quiet but solid as bedrock as I take a step closer. "My *Unseelie* family."

His face tightens. "It was the only way Dahlia would be granted children."

133

"*And she died in childbirth,*" I say coldly, knowing *everything* now. "To her firstborn. Perhaps you should've vetted your sorceress more carefully."

He swallows, something in him crumbling like that might have actually hurt him. "What are you going to do with me, your *grace*?" He places so much on that word.

I turn the healer's pendant in my hand, over and over, as I near a window to peer out into the forest I always wanted to roam. "Nothing I do to you will undo my life." I dip my head down to look at a vase full of fresh dahlias. Of course. I only mattered to *her* because of what a sorceress said I would bring. "No punishment will make my childhood any better. I'm not sure, then, if revenge in a traditional sense is appropriate." I face him, turning around fully to see a scene of armed guards bearing Kane's crest of intertwining thorns surrounding a bear.

"I am going to give you a gilded prison," I continue, staring him down as he tilts his head in confusion. "You will have clothes, food, bedding, and a roof over your head. I'll give you what you gave me." I bend down into a squat, both legs jut to the side to look into his blood-shot eyes. "And I'll make you a *deal*. In ten years, we will accept an offer for your hand in servitude to whoever is willing to pay the highest. I will then receive the offer and decide if I like it or not."

Silas pales. "They'll kill me. Or worse."

"Well then, you'd best behave," I say, echoing his

favorite threat. The same words he used when leaving me with dangerous strangers, expecting me to survive.

"And if they *do* kill me?" His voice is hoarse, frantic.

I rise back to a standing stance, looking down at him with finality. "Then I hope it brings them some peace, just as being with my mate has brought *me* peace."

His eyes flash with disgust, and I know I could twist him to wring out every last bit of remorse, to taste his tears as he realized how much he failed. How stealing me from my home was the beginning of the end for him. But it's a revenge I know will taste emptier and emptier until I'm starving for something I'll never achieve.

I'll *never* recover my childhood.

Turning to walk out of the room, I don't meet Kane's gaze as the Unseelie High Lord stands like a sentinel adorned in his black metal armor. Staring into that silvery gaze will open my vulnerability. I want Silas's last image to be my backside, dressed as perfect and proper as I was raised. Watching him walk away after deflecting my fears was an image that haunted me for *years*.

The halls outside are no less haunted once standing within their sunlight. These walls are forever stained with memories of a small girl who once *yearned* for family.

Kane is not far behind, and when I hear the doors shut, I turn to see the scarred face that has become home for me. Kane's eyes reflect a softness only given to me and those within his family. His roughened hand raises to touch my face, the strength of it something I melt into instantly. His fingers glide down until they find my hair that's now past my breasts. "With your approval, this castle will be turned into a refuge for those who have no home."

I glance down a hall that I would have to traverse to find my way back to the tower—my body stiffens as if overcome with disease, and I yank my gaze right back to Kane's chest, to his sigil inlaid on his chest plate. "Remove the tower," I mumble. "Or seal it off. No one should have to climb that many stairs just to feel alone."

The chest plate moves closer to my face as he leans in to press a kiss on my forehead, my eyes closing as some young part of my soul feels as if her savior *did* come for her.

Maybe all that hope wasn't for nothing.

the end

www.charlottemallory.com
@cmalloryauthor on social media

Kane and Victoria have been alive inside my creativity for some time now, and I decided to give them a novella as an entry into their world. If you loved this book, I have a VERY special hardcover edition with character art, foiling, and beautiful chapter headers on my site, which is listed above.

One day, I'd love to expand their story if there's enough interest. But for now, they feel like they fit perfectly in this bite sized novella.

Please feel free to leave a Goodreads/amazon/book-bub/storygraph review!

My newsletter has all updates, news, character art, etc!

OTHER BOOKS

The Secrets of Jane DUOLOGY.

This is a completed series and also has audiobooks! If Pirates of the Caribbean meets the Witcher is your thing, then you should definitely check this out. Fair warning, it's a world full of improper bastards >:)

I have *many* more books coming, and they'll all entail some version of the same brooding, obsessive MMC.

www.ingramcontent.com/pod-product-compliance
Lightning Source LLC
Chambersburg PA
CBHW072028170626
46811CB00008B/2985